Newcastle
City Council

Newcastle Libraries and Information Service

☎ **0191 277 4100**

2 8 NOV 2015		

Please return this item to any of Newcastle's Libraries by the last date shown above. If not requested by another customer the loan can be renewed, you can do this by phone, post or in person.

Charges may be made for late returns.

Sadie looked down at her hands, damp hair hanging forward across her cheek.

'I'm not the same girl you asked that question all those years ago,' she said, her voice soft.

'You think I don't know that?' he asked. 'Look at me, Sadie.'

She did as he asked, and Dylan took a long moment just absorbing everything she was now. Slowly, obviously, he looked over every inch of her, from her hair—shorter now than when they'd met by a good foot—down over her body, past every added curve and line, every soft patch and every muscle, all the way to her feet.

Did she really not know? Not realise how much she'd grown up since then and how every year had only made her a better person? Who would want the twenty-year-old Sadie compared to the one who sat before him now?

'You are so much more now than you were then,' he murmured, knowing she'd hear him anyway. 'You're stronger, more beautiful, more alive…more than I ever dreamed any woman could be.'

Dear Reader,

A couple of years ago my husband and I were lucky enough to be invited on holiday to Turkey with some very dear friends. It was the first time we'd ever taken our daughter abroad—and the first time I'd left the country since she was born—so we were all very excited.

I knew from our first day in Kusadasi that I needed to set a romance there. There was so much history, scenery and awesome food that I knew it would be perfect. As the week went on it became a bit of a running joke, with everyone pointing out things I could include in my story and coming up with ideas for characters and romantic gestures. I took hundreds and hundreds of photos, along with plenty of notes, so when the time came to write the book I was ready. I just pulled out my photo album and imagined myself back there in the Turkish sun!

I've tried to stay true to the wonderful spirit of the place, and to be as factually accurate as I could—although if I've taken a couple of liberties for the sake of the story I hope you'll forgive me. Most of all, I hope that you enjoy Sadie and Dylan's story as they fumble their way towards happily-ever-after.

Love,

Sophie

A PROPOSAL
WORTH MILLIONS

BY
SOPHIE PEMBROKE

First published in Great Britain 2015
by Mills & Boon, an imprint of Harlequin (UK) Limited,
Eton House, 18-24 Paradise Road, Richmond, Surrey, TW9 1SR

© 2015 Sophie Pembroke

ISBN: 978-0-263-25899-8

Harlequin (UK) Limited's policy is to use papers that are natural,
renewable and recyclable products and made from wood grown in
sustainable forests. The logging and manufacturing processes conform
to the legal environmental regulations of the country of origin.

Printed and bound in Great Britain
by CPI Antony Rowe, Chippenham, Wiltshire

Sophie Pembroke has been reading and writing romance ever since she read her first Mills & Boon romance at university, so getting to write them for a living is a dream come true! Sophie lives in a little Hertfordshire market town in the UK, with her scientist husband and her incredibly imaginative six-year-old daughter. She writes stories about friends, family and falling in love—usually while drinking too much tea and eating homemade cakes. She also keeps a blog at sophiepembroke.com.

For Pete and Kate,
for a truly wonderful, memorable holiday.

CHAPTER ONE

SADIE SULLIVAN BLINKED into the sunshine and waved goodbye to the rental car pulling away from the Azure Hotel. If she squinted, she could just make out Finn's tiny face pressed up against the rear window, and his little hand waving back. Her father, in the driver's seat, was obviously concentrating on the road, but Sadie spotted the glint of her mother's ash-blonde hair beside Finn, and knew she'd be holding him in place, making sure his seat belt was secure.

He was in good hands. She had to remember that. Even if her heart ached at the thought of being separated from her little boy.

The car turned the last corner at the end of the drive and disappeared out of sight, behind the row of juniper trees, onto the road that led up the coast then back inland towards the main roads and Izmir airport. Sadie sucked in a deep breath and wiped the back of her hand across her eyes, quickly, in case anyone was watching. The last thing she needed right now was talk about the boss breaking down in tears. Professionalism, that was the key.

'It's one week, Sullivan,' she muttered to herself. 'Get over yourself. In seven days you'll be in England with him, getting ready to bring him back. Enjoy the peace until then.'

Except next time it might be for longer. A whole term, even. And what if he didn't want to come home to her in the holidays? No, she wasn't thinking about that. Whatever her father said about British schools, about having family around, Finn's place was with her. The local schools were great, and Finn's Turkish was really coming along. He'd be fine.

She swallowed, and stepped back into the coolness of the Azure lobby. Even in late September Kuşadasi still enjoyed the warmth of the Turkish climate. In a few weeks, she knew, the locals would start pulling on sweaters and mumbling about the chill in the air—while she, and the few remaining tourists in town at the end of the season, would still be down at the beach, enjoying the sun.

This time next year Finn would have started school. The only question left to answer definitively was, where?

'Did Finn and your parents leave for the airport okay?' Esma asked, looking up from the reception desk, her long red nails still resting on her keyboard.

Sadie nodded, not trusting herself to speak just yet.

'He's so excited about having a holiday with his grandparents,' Sadie's second in command carried on, regardless. 'And the timing is just perfect, too.'

Sadie kept nodding. Then she blinked. 'It is?'

Esma tilted her head to study her, and Sadie tried to pull herself into her best boss posture and expression. She had the suit, the hair, the make-up—all the things she usually hid behind when she didn't quite know what to do. That armour had got her through her husband's death, through taking on his ridiculously ambitious business project that she didn't have the first clue about. Why on earth would it fail her now, at the prospect of a mere week without her son?

It obviously worked, because Esma shrugged and pushed the work diary across the reception desk towards her.

'I just meant with that potential investor arriving this week. Without Finn to worry about, you will have more time to spend winning him over, yes?'

'Yes, of course,' Sadie responded automatically, her eyes fixed on the red letters spelling 'Investor Visit' written across the next five days. How could she have forgotten?

Her priority for the week. The only thing she had time to worry about, at all, was this investor and all his lovely money.

She hadn't wanted to resort to outside help, but things were getting beyond desperate, even if only she and Neal knew the true extent of the Azure's problems. When their hunt for local investors had failed, Neal had suggested seeking investment from abroad—with similar results. But he'd had a last-chance possibility at the ready when she'd asked where on earth they went next. A business acquaintance, he'd said, who had interests in the hotel industry, and might just be interested enough to send an employee over to check out the Azure.

Sadie had been doubtful, but she was also running out of options. She trusted Neal—he was more than her accountant, he had been one of her late husband Adem's best friends. And she had no doubt that Neal would have asked his acquaintance to go easy on her. Everyone always did.

She's a widow. They always shook their head sadly as they said the word 'widow'. *Lost her husband in a car crash, tragically young.*

These days, that was often the only thing people knew about her at all. Well, that and the fact that she was saddled with a white elephant of a hotel renovation that might never be finished at the rate things were going.

Sadie was almost sure there used to be more to know about her once.

Behind the reception desk Esma's eyes were wide and worried, so Sadie reinforced her 'in control of everything' smile. She had to shake off the negativity. She loved the Azure, just like Adem had, and just like Finn did. It was her home, and she would make it a success—one way or another.

She'd made promises. Commitments. And she had every intention of fulfilling them.

She just might have to accept a little help along the way.

'Did Neal call with the name of the guy the company is sending over yet?' Sadie asked. 'And we have a car collecting him from the airport, correct?'

'Yes, at four o'clock,' Esma confirmed. 'I sent Alim.'

'Good.' Alim was reliable, and his English was great—far better than her Turkish, even after four years of living in the country and working hard to learn. Finn was a much quicker study than her, it turned out.

And just like that, she'd forgotten all her business worries again and was back to fretting about her son. Part of being a mother, she supposed.

She checked her watch. It was already gone five.

'Has Alim texted to say they're on their way?' Sadie asked.

'Almost an hour ago. They should be here any moment.' Esma bit her lip. 'It will all be fine, Sadie,' she added after a moment. But it sounded more like a question than reassurance.

Sadie smiled broadly. 'Of course it will! I'm certain of it,' she lied. Then something occurred to her. Esma had only answered half her question. 'And the name?' she pressed. 'Neal gave it to you, yes?' How embarrassing would it be to greet this guy with no idea what to call him?

Behind the desk, Esma squirmed, shuffling an irrelevant stack of papers between her hands, her gaze fixed firmly on her nails. Something heavy settled in Sadie's stomach at the sight. Something heavier even than her guilt about Finn being away all week. Something more like the magnitude of the fears and nightmares that kept her awake at night, wondering how on earth she would achieve everything she'd promised her husband and son.

'Esma? What's his name?'

Her face pale, Esma finally looked up to meet Sadie's gaze. 'Neal said it might be better if you…' She trailed off.

'If I what?' Sadie asked. 'Didn't know the name of the person who might hold the future of this place in his hands? Why on earth would he—? Unless…'

Behind her, she heard the swoosh of the automatic doors and the clunk of a heavy suitcase on the marble floors. Her heart beat in double time, and that heavy feeling spread up through her chest, constricting her breathing and threatening her poor, laboured heart.

Sadie turned, and suddenly it was thirteen years ago. She could almost sense Adem beside her—younger, more nervous, but alive—hopping from foot to foot as he introduced his new girlfriend to his two best friends. Neal Stephens and Dylan Jacobs.

Except Adem was dead, Neal was in England—where she couldn't yell at him yet—and only Dylan stood in the lobby of her hotel. Dylan, who was supposed to be thousands of miles away in Australia, where he belonged. Instead, he was at the Azure, as self-assured and cocky as ever. And every inch as handsome.

No wonder Neal hadn't told her. She'd have been on

the first flight out with Finn, and he knew it. He might not know everything, but Neal had to at least have noticed that she'd made a concerted effort *not* to see Dylan since the funeral.

But now she couldn't run. She had commitments to keep—and she needed Dylan Jacobs of all people to help her do that.

Sadie plastered on a smile, stepped forward, and held out a hand that only shook a bit.

'Dylan! How wonderful to see you again,' she said, and prayed it didn't sound like the lie it was.

Dylan's chest tightened automatically at the sight of her. An hour's drive from the airport and hours on the plane before that, and he still wasn't ready. In fact, as he stepped forward to take Sadie's hand he realised he might never be ready. Not for this.

Five minutes ago he'd been moments away from calling the whole visit off. Sitting in the car, as they'd come up the long, winding hotel driveway, he'd almost told the driver to turn around and take him back to the airport. That the whole trip was a mistake.

But Dylan Jacobs never shied away from an opportunity. And, besides, it was Sadie. So instead he'd checked his phone again—emails first, then messages, then voicemails then other alerts—his habitual order. Anything to distract him from thinking about Sadie.

He hadn't seen her in two years. Two long years since the funeral. Hadn't even heard a peep from her—let alone a response to his card, telling her to call, if she ever needed anything.

And now, apparently, she needed everything and she was calling in that promise.

He just wished she'd done it in person, instead of via

Neal. Wished he could have spoken to her, heard her voice, sensed her mood.

Wished he had a better idea what he was walking into here.

She's coping, Neal had said. *Better than a lot of people would. But...she lost Adem, Dyl. Of course she's not the same. And she needs you. The Azure is all she has left of her husband, and you can help her save it.*

So in a rapid flurry of emails Dylan had been booked on the next plane into Izmir and now there he was. At Adem's dream hotel. With Adem's dream woman.

Glancing at the sign above the hotel doors, Dylan had winced at the name. The Azure. Why did it have to be that name? There were a hundred perfectly decent generic hotel names on offer. Why on earth had Adem picked that one?

A half-forgotten memory had flashed through his brain. Adem's excited phone call, telling him all about his next big project, how he and Sadie were moving to Turkey to save some ramshackle old hotel that had once belonged to his Turkish mother's grandfather or something. What he remembered most was the sharp sting that had hit his chest at the name—and the utter irrationality of it.

It's just a name. It doesn't mean anything, he'd reminded himself.

But symbolism was a bitch, and to Dylan the Azure would always mean loss. The loss of his father, his freedom, so many years ago. Loss of hope. Lost chances and opportunities.

Except maybe, just maybe, this time it could be different. So much had changed... And this was a different hotel, thousands of miles and more than two decades away from the Azure where the man who had raised him had walked out on his entire family and never looked back.

This was Sadie's hotel now.

He'd never told Adem the whole story of his father, and had certainly never mentioned the name of the hotel. If he had, his friend would probably have changed it, just to make Dylan feel more comfortable. That was the sort of man Adem had been, the good, caring, thoughtful sort.

The sort of man who had deserved the love of a woman like Sadie.

Unbidden, images of the last time he'd seen her had filled Dylan's vision. Dressed all in black, instead of the bright colours she'd always loved, standing beside that coffin in a cold, rainy, English graveyard. She'd been gripping her tiny son's hand, he remembered, and he'd known instinctively that if she'd had her way Finn wouldn't have been there, wouldn't have had to witness any of it. He'd wondered who had insisted he take part, and how lost Sadie must have been to let them win.

Lost. That was the right word for it. She'd looked small and tired and sad…but most of all she'd looked lost. As if without Adem she'd had no compass any more, no path.

It had broken Dylan's heart to see her that way. But standing outside her hotel…he had just wondered who she would be now.

And then it was time to find out.

Heart racing, he climbed the steps to the hotel entrance and let the automatic doors sweep back to allow him in. He squinted in the relative cool darkness of the lobby, compared to the bright sunlight outside. But when his vision cleared the first thing he saw was Sadie—standing at the reception desk, her back turned to him so he couldn't make out her face. But there was never any doubt in his mind that it was her, despite the plain grey suit and shorter hair.

So many memories were buttoned up in that suit—of the friend he'd lost and the woman he'd never even had a chance with—that his chest tightened just at the sight of her.

He braced himself as she turned, but it wasn't enough. Nowhere near enough to prepare him for the shock and horror that flashed across her familiar face, before she threw up a pleasant, smiling mask to cover it.

She didn't know I was coming. Oh, he was going to *kill* Neal. Painfully, and probably slowly.

Reflex carried him through the moment, the old defences leaping back into place as she smiled and held out her hand. Her hand. Like they really were new business acquaintances, instead of old friends.

'Dylan! How wonderful to see you again,' she said, still smiling through the obvious lie. And Dylan wished that, for once, he'd ignored the opportunity and headed back to the airport like his gut had told him to.

But it was too late now.

Ignoring the sting of her lie, Dylan took her cool fingers between his own, tugging her closer until he could wrap his other arm around her slim waist, his fingers sliding up from hers to circle her wrist and keep her close. Just the touch of her sent his senses into overdrive, and he swallowed hard before speaking.

'It's so good to see you, Sadie.' And that, at least, was the truth. Dylan could feel his world move back into balance at the sight of her and the feel of her in his arms… well, it just told him what he'd known for years. That the feelings for his best friend's girl he'd tried so hard to bury had never been hidden all that deep at all.

He really was going to kill Neal for this.

Sadie pulled back, still smiling, apparently unaware of how his world had just shifted alignment again, the same way it had thirteen years ago when Adem had said, 'Dyl, this is Sadie. She's…special,' and Sadie's cheeks had turned pink as she'd smiled.

A real smile, that had been. Not at all like the one she gave him now.

'Let's get you checked in,' Sadie said, and Dylan nodded.

Even though he knew the most sensible thing to do would be to run, as far and as fast as he could, away from the Azure Hotel.

Maybe his dad had had the right idea after all.

Sadie's hands shook as she climbed the stairs to her tiny office—the one that used to be Adem's—and reached for the door handle. Instinctively, she checked back over her shoulder to make sure Dylan hadn't followed her. But, no, the stairs were clear and she was alone at last, and able to process what had already been a difficult day.

Hopefully by now Dylan would be happily ensconced in the best suite the Azure had to offer—which was probably still nowhere near the standard he was used to. He hadn't let her escape without making her promise to meet him for dinner, though. Of course, she'd said yes—she was hardly in a position to say no, now, was she? She just hoped he had no idea how much she'd wanted to.

Stepping into her office, she slumped into her desk chair and reached for the phone, her fingers still trembling. Dialling the familiar number, she let it ring, waiting for Neal to pick up. He'd be there, she was sure, waiting by the phone. After all, he had to know she'd be calling.

'I'm sorry,' Neal said, the moment he answered.

'So you bloody well should be. What were you think-

ing? Why didn't you tell me? Never mind, I think I know.'
Which didn't make her any happier about the subterfuge.
Not one bit.

'You'd have said no,' Neal explained anyway. 'But,
Sadie, he really wants to help. And you need him.'

'I *don't* need a pity save.' Sadie could feel the heat
of her anger rising again and let it come. Neal deserved
it. 'I'm not some bank that's too big to fail. I don't need
Dylan Jacobs to sweep in and—'

'Yes,' Neal said, calm but firm. 'You do. And you
know it.'

Yes, she did. But she wished that wasn't true.

'Why did it have to be him, though?' she whined.

'Who else do we know with millions of pounds, a tendency to jump at random opportunities and a soft spot
for your family?' Neal teased lightly.

'True.' Didn't mean she had to like it, though.
Although Neal was right about the jumping-at-
opportunities thing. Dylan was the ultimate opportunist
and once he'd jumped it was never long before he
was ready to move on to the next big thing. This
wasn't a long-term project for him, Sadie realised.
This was Dylan swooping in just long enough to give
her a hand, then he'd be moving on. She needed to
remember that.

'Is this really a problem?' Neal asked. 'I mean, I knew
your pride would be a bit bent out of shape, but you told
me you wanted to save the Azure, come hell or high water.'

She had said that. 'Which is this, exactly?'

There was a pause on the other end of the line, and
Sadie began to regret the joke. The last thing she needed
on top of Dylan Jacobs in her hotel was Neal showing up
to find out what was going on.

'Why does he bother you so much?' He sounded honestly curious, like he was trying to riddle out the mystery of Sadie and Dylan. The same way Neal always approached everything—like a puzzle to be solved. It was one of the things Sadie liked most about him. He'd taken the problem of her failing hotel and had started looking for answers, rather than pointing out things she'd done wrong. 'It can't be that he reminds you of Adem too much or you'd have kicked me to the kerb after the funeral, too. So what is it?'

Sadie sighed. There was just no way to explain this that Neal would ever understand. His riddle would have to go unsolved. 'I don't know. We just…we never really managed to see eye to eye. On anything.'

Except for that one night, when they'd seen each other far too clearly. When she'd finally realised the threat that Dylan Jacobs had posed to her carefully ordered and settled life.

The threat of possibility.

'He's a good man,' Neal told her. 'He really does want to help.'

'I know.' That was the worst part. Dylan wasn't here to cause trouble, or make her life difficult, or unhappy. She knew him well enough to be sure of that. He was there to help, probably out of some misguided sense of obligation to a man who was already two years dead, and the friendship they'd shared. She could respect that. 'And I need him. I should have called him myself.' She thought of the sympathy card sitting with a few others in a drawer in her bedroom. The one with a single lily on the front and stark, slashing black handwriting inside.

I'm so sorry, Sadie. Whatever you need, call me.
Any time.
D x.

She hadn't, obviously.

'So we're okay?' Neal asked.

'Yeah, Neal. We're fine.' It was only her own sanity she was worried about. 'I'll call you later in the week, let you know how things go.'

'Okay.' Neal still sounded uncertain, but he hung up anyway when she said goodbye.

Sadie leant back in her chair, tipping her head to stare at the ceiling. All she needed to do was find a way to work with Dylan until he moved on to the next big thing—and from past experience that wouldn't take long. Jobs, businesses, women—none of them had ever outlasted his short boredom threshold. Why would the Azure be any different? The only thing Sadie had ever known to be constant in Dylan's life was his friendship with Adem and Neal. That was all this was about—a feeling of obligation to his friend, and the wife and child he'd left behind. She didn't need him, she needed his money and his business.

A niggle of guilt wriggled in her middle at the realisation that she was basically using her husband's best friend for his money, milking his own sense of loss at Adem's death. But if it was the only way to save the Azure…

She'd convince him that the Azure was worth saving, and he'd stump up the money out of obligation.

Then they could both move on.

CHAPTER TWO

DYLAN WAITED A while before calling Neal to yell at him. After all, he figured he owed Sadie a fair crack at their mutual friend first.

In the meantime, the wait gave him the opportunity to settle into his suite, his frequent flyer business traveller mind assessing the space the way he always did in a new hotel room. Bed: king-size—always a good start. The linens were crisp and white, and part of his weary brain and body wanted to curl up in them right away and sleep until dinner. But he was there to do a job, and that job required him to be awake, so he pushed on.

The room itself was a good size, but Dylan figured this was probably the biggest the hotel had, so he'd have to explore some of the smaller, ordinary rooms before making a judgement on room size. Wandering through to the bathroom, he clocked fluffy towels, good tiling and lighting, and a shower he very much looked forward to trying out later. If that shower head was as effective as it looked, and the water pressure as good as Dylan hoped, his aching muscles would appreciate the pummelling before bed.

Back in the main room, Dylan ran his fingers across the small table and chairs by the window in the bedroom then strolled into the lounge area through the open arch of a doorway. Again, the size was good, the sofas looked comfy enough, and the coffee table was stacked with magazines and brochures detailing things to do in the area. He flicked through them quickly before deciding the mini-bar and desk were far more interesting.

Crouching down, he yanked open the fridge door and nodded his approval. A decently stocked mini-bar—even if he never used it—was a must in Dylan's book. Then he dropped into the swivel chair by the desk, tugged his phone from his pocket and checked for the complementary WiFi the girl at the desk had assured him was part of his room package. To his amazement, it worked first time and with minimal fuss over the password.

He smiled to himself. He shouldn't be so surprised. After all, this was Adem's place, for all that Sadie was running it now. And Adem had always been vocal about the individual's right to easy-access WiFi at all times and in all places. Something else he and Dylan had always agreed on.

Twirling around in his chair, Dylan split his attention between checking his mail again and surveying the room as a whole—and spotted something he hadn't noticed before. Getting to his feet, he crossed the room, pulled aside the curtains and stepped out onto the suite's small balcony.

Now this was worth travelling all those miles for. Breathing in deeply, Dylan savoured the warm sun on his face and forearms, and stared out. He could see now why Adem had been so evangelical about the place, right from the start, quite apart from his family connection to the hotel.

The view was magnificent. Down below, the Aegean Sea lapped against the rocks, bright and blue and entrancing, sending up puffs of white spray with every wave. Above the rocks, scrubby bushes and juniper trees twisted up towards the clear azure sky, all the way up the peak where the hotel sat. Overhead, a bird called out as it passed, and Dylan thought for the first time all year, since he spent the holidays with his sister and her family, that he might actually be able to just switch off and enjoy the moment.

Except he still had to deal with Sadie—and find out how bad things at the Azure really were for Neal to have sent him here when she so obviously didn't want his help.

Eventually, he figured enough time had passed that even Sadie would have finished yelling at the hapless accountant and, leaving the sunny warmth of the balcony behind him, Dylan headed back inside to sit at the desk and call Neal.

After just a couple of rings Neal answered the phone with a sigh.

'You can't possibly be surprised by this call,' Dylan pointed out.

'I know, I know.' Neal sounded stressed, in a way Dylan wasn't used to hearing from his old friend. That alone put his nerves on high alert. 'Trust me, I've already heard it all from her.'

Her. Sadie. The memory of her expression, the shock and horror that had flashed across her face at the first sight of him, rankled all over again.

'I bet you have,' Dylan said. 'So? Is she going to kick me out on my ear or let me help?' It wasn't what he'd expected to ask—he'd expected there to be a lot more yelling first, apart from anything else. But now he had Neal on the phone it seemed like the only thing that really mattered.

'She'll let you help.'

'Because she's desperate.'

'Pretty much.'

'Great.' Dylan put as much sarcasm as he could muster into the word. 'I just love being a last resort.'

Neal let out another, world-weary sigh. 'You know Sadie, Dyl. She's proud. And she thinks it's her responsibility to fulfil Adem's dreams all on her own.'

'She let *you* help.' Which, Dylan had to admit, still irked him a bit.

'Yeah, but I'm less smug than you.'

Smug? 'I'm not—'

'Yes. Yes, you are. And you need not to be this week, okay?' Neal wasn't joking any more, Dylan could tell. And that worried him more than anything else that had happened that day.

But, to be honest, being too smug and alienating Sadie wasn't really what Dylan was concerned about. He was far more worried about being obvious than smug. Worried that Sadie still thought she knew more about his feelings than she could reasonably expect to after so many years—and might refuse to let him help because of it.

'Things are that bad here?' he asked.

Neal huffed impatiently, a far more familiar sound than his concern. 'Didn't you read the info I sent over?'

'Of course I did.' Well, he'd scanned through it on the plane, which was practically the same thing. It wasn't that Dylan wasn't interested in the stats for the Azure Hotel, it was just that he had a lot of other projects on his plate, plus new opportunities coming in. Besides... he hadn't really been able to imagine any of it until he was actually here.

'She needs more than your money, Dyl. She needs your business brain.'

And, okay, yes, it was bad timing, but it wasn't really

his fault that his brain's automatic response to a comment like that was a feeling of smug pride, right? 'Doesn't everyone?'

'Okay, that? That's exactly what I don't want you to do this week.'

The puff of pride disintegrated as fast as it had appeared. 'Fine. So I'm here in a business advisor capacity only?'

'No, she needs your money, too,' Neal said. 'She's insanely committed to Adem's dream of making the Azure a successful hotel. Doesn't matter that he's not there to see it—she's going to make it happen anyway.'

Only Sadie. Other people walked out on commitments every day—families, marriages, financial and business obligations—and never looked back. Only Sadie would remain committed to a dead man's schemes. And only because she had loved Adem so much.

Dylan sighed. 'That's not going to be easy.' He knew that much from the information Neal had sent him—and the fact Sadie had agreed to let him help at all. If she'd thought she could do it herself, she would have. Sadie was nothing if not bloody-minded and determined.

'Probably not,' Neal allowed. 'But it might save Adem's dream. And Sadie.'

And so, of course, he would do it, without question. He just hoped no one ever pressed him to say exactly which of those motivations was strongest for him.

'I'm having dinner with her tonight.' He tugged a sheet of writing paper branded with the Azure logo closer to him and grabbed a pen. 'Where do I start?'

'She needs this to be business,' Neal said. 'Not a pity save, even if that's what it is.'

It was more than that, Dylan knew. This wasn't just pity. He couldn't bear to see Sadie struggling, so he'd do whatever it took to save her. He suspected that Neal knew that too.

'So how do I convince her it's not?'

'By letting her pitch the Azure and Kuşadasi to you as a real investment opportunity. As something you'd want to put money into even if she wasn't involved. Let her present her proposal for the place, then decide if you will invest.'

Suddenly, a plan began to form, right at the back of Dylan's brain, where he always got his most inspired ideas.

'I can do that,' he said, and smiled.

Standing in front of her wardrobe, Sadie shifted her weight from one foot to the other, squinted, then sighed and gave up. Nothing she could do right now changed the clothes hanging there for her to choose from. If Neal had told her Dylan was coming, she'd have had time to go shopping. Not that she would have done. The last thing she wanted to do was give Dylan Jacobs the impression that his presence was new-clothes-worthy.

Either way, her options now were limited.

She flicked through the hangers again, dismissing each outfit in turn. Black suit? Too conservative for dinner with someone who was, business opportunities aside, an old friend. Navy shift dress? Might have worked, if it didn't have hummus smeared down the front of it, courtesy of Finn. She tossed it in the laundry hamper. Grey shift dress? She supposed it could work. The neckline was demure, the fit okay... It was just boring and made her look even greyer than she felt.

Hadn't she once had more interesting clothes? The sort with colour and pop and stuff? She was sure that once upon a time she'd dressed to fit her happy and in-love mood. Maybe that was the problem. When Adem had died he'd taken all her colour and brightness with him—and it even showed in her wardrobe.

Trapping her lower lip between her teeth, Sadie reached right to the back of the closet and felt slippery satin slide through her fingers as she tugged one more dress to the front. *The* dress. The bright red, sexy dress her sister had talked her into buying on their last shopping trip to London before she and Adem had left for Turkey. She'd never yet found the courage to wear it, for all of Rachel's suggestions that it would be the perfect dress to wear if she wanted to convince Adem they should give Finn a little brother or sister.

She let it fall from her grasp. Definitely *not* the right dress for tonight.

Instead, she pulled out her standard black function dress—the one she'd worn for every single event since she'd arrived in Kuşadasi, and the dress she'd known she'd end up wearing all along, if she was honest with herself. It was well cut, didn't reveal too much, looked more dressy than a work dress, but still had the aura of business about it.

Sadie sank to sit on her bed, her hands clutching at the fabric of the dress. Business. She had to focus on that. This was her last and only chance—she couldn't afford to think of Dylan as Adem's twenty-two-year-old university buddy, or the best man who'd brought Adem home from his stag night with an almighty hangover, a blow-up sheep and no recollection of where they'd spent the last two days. Dylan wasn't that person any more.

She swallowed, blinking away sudden tears of guilt and loss at the memory of her husband. Because that was the problem. She wasn't thinking of *that* Dylan at all. Instead, she couldn't help remembering another one, sitting up too late in a bar after someone else's wedding, talking too much and too deeply.

Despite herself, she couldn't help remembering the man who had once asked her if she'd ever imagined what might have happened if he'd met her first, instead of Adem.

Rushing to her feet, too fast, Sadie shook off the memory with the resulting light-headedness. She loved her husband—now, then and always. And she planned to preserve his memory for their son by saving the hotel. Business, that's all any of it was for her now. And she was sure that was all it was for Dylan too.

She knew business now, and she needed to show Dylan that—needed him to see that she wasn't the same girl she had been then either. She'd grown up, learned and changed. She could save the Azure all by herself—she just needed his money.

Nodding to herself, Sadie pulled on her black dress and added her work jacket and heels. A business-casual compromise, she decided. It was perfect.

Heading down to the bar, Sadie was pleased to realise she'd beaten Dylan there, despite her clothing dilemma delay. After a moment's thought she ordered them both a glass of a local white wine—showcasing the specialties of the region had to be a good way to convince Dylan that Kuşadasi was worth his time and interest. Following her theme, she also asked the bartender to check in with the chef on the menu. He returned in short order, carrying both wine and a daily menu. Sadie scanned it quickly and told him to instruct the chef to serve them both the best local food on offer, once they made it through to the restaurant.

She settled back onto her bar stool and took a sip of her wine, feeling in control for the first time that day. Dylan may have caught her off balance when he'd arrived, but it took more than that to rattle Sadie Sullivan. She had everything in hand now—and it was the upper one.

Then he appeared in the doorway, looking far too good in his navy suit and open-collared shirt, and she struggled to swallow her wine without spluttering. Dylan, Sadie was sure, hadn't bothered agonising over what to wear at all. He'd just thrown on what he liked and looked… *perfect* in it.

It was strange; she didn't remember him being quite so attractive. Oh, he'd always been good looking, but it had been in a single-guy-about-town, flirt-with-the-girls-and-take-them-home way. Whereas Adem had always been more steady, less striking—but so gorgeous when he'd smiled at her. It had felt like he'd saved all his best looks just for her, and she'd loved that.

But now Dylan looked more grown up, more reliable, like he'd grown into his looks and out of his bad habits. Sadie shook her head lightly—it was an illusion. She knew from Neal's more recent stories that Dylan was just as much of a playboy as ever.

'You look beautiful.' Reaching her stool, Dylan bent to kiss her cheek, and Sadie ignored the thrill it sent down her spine.

'And you're just as much of a flirt as ever,' she chastised him, earning the reward of a positively rakish grin that made it hard not to laugh. 'Have a seat,' she said, waving at the stool next to her. 'Drink wine.'

He did as he was told for once, fishing his smartphone from his pocket and placing it on the bar before he reached for his glass.

'This is good,' Dylan said, after the first mouthful. 'Local?'

She nodded. 'Everything you're going to taste tonight is from the area. Just another host of reasons why you want to be investing in Kuşadası and the Azure.'

'Down to business so soon?' His smile was a little lop-sided this time, like he knew something she didn't, but since he was already swiping a finger across his phone screen to check his emails Sadie didn't think he should complain about talking business in a bar.

'Isn't that what you're here for?' Best to be blunt, she decided. History aside, this was a business dinner—for both of them.

'Of course.' Dylan leant against the wooden back of the bar stool, his arms folded behind his head. 'Go on, then. I'm ready to be convinced.'

'About the food?' Sadie asked, suddenly thrown off balance. Surely he didn't expect her to convince him to invest a ridiculous amount of money based purely on one sip of wine and the promise of dinner?

'About this hotel. You're right, this is a business trip. As much as I'd personally be happy to hand over what-ever money you need, I have shareholders and board members who might not be so keen. So I need you to convince me that the Azure is a sound investment be-fore I can agree to come on board.' His tone was per-fectly matter-of-fact, even as he admitted he'd give her a pity save if he could. A very small part of Sadie wished it was that easy.

But no. This was exactly what she'd wanted—no pity save, no charity for the poor widow. Business.

She just hadn't expected him to agree so fast—or for it to be a requirement for him too.

But she could do this. She could show him. She had a

plan—Adem's plan for the Azure—and she intended to follow it to the letter. All she needed to do was convince Dylan it was a good plan.

'Right, then,' she said, briskly. 'Where do you want to start?'

CHAPTER THREE

THE MOMENT THEY were settled at their table—obviously the best seat in the house—Sadie launched into what had to be a rehearsed sales pitch. Dylan tried to pay attention as she listed the details of room numbers and styles, amenities and so on, but in truth very little of it went in. He couldn't keep his eyes off her—and apparently he'd lost the ability to stare and listen at the same time.

Sadie was beautiful as ever, he'd known that since he arrived at the Azure. Before, even. Sadie was Sadie, and her beauty was an intrinsic part of her—and had very little to do with what she actually looked like at all. But now, soaking her in over the candlelit table, he had a chance to catalogue the changes. She was more fragile now, he decided, more closed off. Somehow more off limits than she'd ever been, even after she'd married Adem. Now she was The Widow, and he couldn't seem to help but let those two words—and the tragedy they encompassed—define her in his mind.

Her spark seemed dimmed, and it hurt him to see it. Maybe this week could be useful in more than one way. He'd help her with her hotel, of course. But how could he not try to bring that spark back too? To make sure she was really okay here, alone with a crumbling hotel, a small boy and her memories.

Just as a friend. Obviously. Because there was no way she'd let him close enough for anything else now, if she never had before. Besides, given the position she was in, he wouldn't risk it. Not if it would just make things worse for her. All he had to offer was the money she needed and business support maybe. Then he would be on his way. He wasn't Adem and he never had been.

Dylan knew himself too well—at least as well as Neal, Adem and Sadie always had. He was too like his father to ever settle to one life, one set of possibilities—not when the next big thing could be just past the horizon. So this was temporary, and that was fine with him.

It just meant he only had one week to find the promise in the Azure Hotel and come up with a plan to make it good. He needed to get started on that, pronto. *Priorities, Dylan.*

Their starters arrived without him ever seeing a menu, but as he examined the seafood platter he decided he didn't mind at all. If all else failed, at least he could honestly say the food and drink at the Azure were good. It was a start.

'Did Adem make you memorise all that?' he asked, as Sadie reached the end of her spiel and reached for a calamari ring.

'No,' she said. 'Well, just some of it.'

'But it's all his plan, right?' He'd known Adem since they'd been eighteen. He'd recognised his friend's touch before Sadie had reached the second bullet point.

'How can you possibly…? We worked on it together. Of course.'

'Of course. But this was his dream.' He followed her lead with the calamari, hoping it tasted as good as it looked. One piece of rubbery calamari could ruin a whole meal. But, no, it had the perfect mixture of crunch in the batter and melting seafood. He reached for another.

'His heritage.' She shrugged, her shoulders slim and delicate now she'd taken her jacket off, and more tanned than he remembered. 'He wanted a future here for our family.'

Family. *Stop thinking about her shoulders, Jacobs, and focus on what really matters to her.* 'Where *is* Finn, anyway?'

A shadow crossed her face, and he almost regretted asking. 'He's staying with my parents for the week. I'm flying over to England to collect him after you leave.'

'Because I was going to be here?' That stung. He may not have seen much of the boy since he'd been born, but that didn't make him any less of an honorary uncle.

Sadie gave him a look—the sort she used to give him in the pub when they'd been twenty-two and he'd been acting like an idiot. 'To be honest, I didn't know *you* were the one coming, which I think you must have guessed. Besides, that wasn't it. He's due to start school next year, and my parents wanted to spend some time with him outside the holidays before then.'

There was something else, hiding behind the lightness of her tone, but he couldn't put his finger on it, and it was still too early to press too hard for information—frustrating as that was. He had to have patience. Eventually she'd open up to him again.

A waiter cleared their starter platters, even as another brought their main course—some sort of delicious, spicy, lamb stew thing that Dylan vowed to find out the name of before he left. But right then he had bigger priorities than his stomach.

'Okay, so, I've heard all the grand plans,' he said between mouthfuls. 'How far have you actually got with them?'

Sadie put down her fork and ticked the items off on her fingers as she spoke. 'The lobby, restaurant and bar are finished, as you've seen. So is the spa. Of the bedrooms, the top floor with the penthouse suite—your suite—and the other family suites is done, and the first floor of luxury doubles.'

'So that leaves you, what?' He tried to recall the floor numbers from the lift. 'Another four floors to go? Plus any other reception and function rooms?'

She nodded. 'We had a timescale planned but…'

'The money ran out.' Not a surprise. He'd seen it often enough, even in projects less plagued by tragedy and uncertainty.

'Yes. So we opened anyway, to try and get enough funds to keep going. But at least one of the floors is uninhabitable as it stands, so occupancy is never very high.'

'What about the outside space?' That had to be a selling point in a climate like this.

'The outside pool needs retiling and the path down to the beach needs some work. Fortunately the inside pool is attached to the spa, so got done in the first wave, before…' She trailed off, and he knew exactly what she wasn't saying. Some days, he thought that if he didn't say it, it might not be true, too.

'There's a lot left to do,' he finished for her, cutting short the moment.

'That's why we need your money.'

His fork hit china and he looked down to see he'd eaten the whole bowl without tasting anything beyond that first delicious mouthful. What a waste. He put his cutlery down. 'Dinner would be worth investing in alone. That was truly delicious.'

She blushed, just a little. 'I'm glad you enjoyed it. Somehow I suspect one meal isn't quite enough to win over your shareholders, though.'

'Maybe not. Okay, listen. I'm going to tell you a bit about my company, and you can decide if you want us involved. If you do…then we can discuss what else I need to see and do, what questions I need answered, before I can take a proposal to the board.' She'd been straight with him, as far as he could tell. Time for him to do the same.

'Okay.' Eyes wide, her nerves were back, he realised, pleased to still be able to read her so well.

'My company isn't generally interested in long-term investment. Mostly what we do is take on a failing business, tear it down or build it up until it's successful, then sell it on.'

'In that case, I'd think the Azure would be perfect. We have "failing business" written all over us.' She reached for her wine—a local red, he assumed—and took a gulp.

'The key is, the business has to have the *potential* to be a huge success,' he clarified. 'In the right hands.'

'Yours, you mean.' She sounded more sceptical than Dylan felt was truly necessary.

'Or whoever we put in charge. In this case…we'd need to be sure that you could turn this place around on your own, with just money and guidance from us.' Make it clear upfront that he wouldn't be staying around—not that he imagined she wanted him to.

'I see.' This time her tone gave nothing away at all, and he found himself talking just to fill the silence that followed.

'Unless, of course, you're in favour of taking a bulldozer to the place, putting someone else in charge of the rebuild and taking a back seat until the money starts rolling in?' He knew she wouldn't say yes, but part of him couldn't help but hope she would. It would be the easy way out—but since when had Sadie ever taken that?

She shook her head. 'Sorry. This is personal for me. I made a commitment to make this hotel a success. For Adem.'

'I guessed you'd say that. Don't suppose you'd consider changing the name either?'

'No,' she said, giving him a curious look. 'Why? What's wrong with the name it has?'

'No reason.' She stared and waited. He sighed. He should have known that wasn't a good enough answer for her. 'I had a bad experience at an Azure Hotel once.'

Her wide grin made the admission worthwhile. 'Let me guess. Some woman's poor husband showed up at the wrong moment?'

Of course that's what she would think. And, really, who could blame her? 'You know me.' But not all his secrets—which was probably for the best. For both of them.

'Okay, so if we're not going to knock this place down, what do I need to show you to convince you we're worth your time, money and effort?'

Honestly, he could probably make the decision based purely on the numbers. But that would have him flying back to Sydney tomorrow, instead of spending time with Sadie. He had to give her a real chance to convince him.

'Here's my proposal. I want a proper tour of the hotel. Then I need to see the local area—get a feel for the economy and tourist potential. Numbers are all well and good, but you need to visit a place to get a real feeling for it.' All true, up to a point. 'Then we'll sit down together and see if I can help you save this place.'

She nodded. 'Okay. Do you want me to set you up with the local tour company we use?'

Where would be the fun in that? 'No. I think this will

work much better if you show me yourself.' Not to mention give him a clearer idea of how Sadie was really coping after her husband's death. Multitasking was the key to any successful business, after all.

Sadie nodded her agreement, and Dylan sat back to anticipate dessert, hoping his smile wasn't too smug. Everything was going to plan.

After a restless night, full of dreams that were half memory, half fantasy, Sadie met Dylan in the lobby the next morning, dressed in her best black suit and determined to impress with her business skills. His proposal had been more than fair. Neal must have told him what dire straits they were in at the Azure, but still Dylan had agreed to spend time on the ground, studying and evaluating everything himself, before he made his decision.

Sadie suspected that had more to do with friendship than good business sense. Still, he'd made it very clear over dinner what he needed from her—professionalism—and she intended to give it to him in spades.

Except Dylan, when he arrived, was dressed in light trousers and a pale blue shirt with the sleeves rolled up, sunglasses tucked in his pocket, making her feel instantly overdressed—even though *she* was the one who was appropriately attired. *How does he* always *manage that?*

'Right, let's get going,' he said, as he approached. 'Lots to see today!'

'Before we start our tour,' she said, stalling him, 'I realised there was something I forgot to show you yesterday, and I'd hate you to miss it.'

Striding across the lobby, she led him to the windows at the far side of the elevators. Dylan wasn't the sort to stop and sniff the roses, unless someone reminded him to, and she couldn't have him missing the most magnificent thing about the Azure, just because he forgot to look.

'Oh, really? What's that?' Dylan asked, following, his eyes on the screen of his smartphone.

'Our view.' Sadie stared out across the bright blue waters, the sea almost the same colour as the sky, white foam echoing the wispy clouds overhead. They were high enough to see for miles, out along the coast and out to sea. Her heart tightened the way it always did when she looked out over the water and coast beyond the Azure. Whatever had happened here, she was lucky to have had the chance to live in such a beautiful country. She had to remember that.

'There's a path from the back door that leads straight down to the beach,' she murmured, but Dylan's eyes remained fixed on the view, just as she'd known they would.

It was this view that Adem had used to convince her, back when buying a crumbling hotel had just been a pipe dream.

Look at it, he'd said. *Who wouldn't want to be here?*

And in that moment she hadn't been able to imagine anywhere she'd rather be than in the Azure Hotel, making Adem's dreams a reality.

Dylan looked similarly entranced, his phone forgotten in his hand. Sadie allowed herself a small smile. Perhaps this would be easier than she'd thought.

'Of course, the view would still be there, even if you knocked this old place down and rebuilt it,' he said, turning his back on the view, but his tone told her he was joking. Mostly. 'You could put in a whole glass wall in the lobby, and rooms with a sea view could have folding glass doors and balconies. Really make the most of the asset—and change the name while you're at it...'

Sadie rolled her eyes. Some woman—or her husband—had really done a number on him in an Azure Hotel, hadn't she? Funny that Adem or Neal had never told her that story, when they'd shared so many others.

Was that why he couldn't see it? The romance of this place? This old building was more than just its stones and its view. It was the heart of the place.

'Time for the rest of our tour, then. But I want you to remember—this is all business.' Sure, he'd said it himself the night before, but it couldn't hurt to hammer the point home. 'I want you to treat me and the Azure like you would any other business proposition. We're here to impress you, our client. So, what do you want to see first?'

'I'm the client, huh? My wish is your command. Sounds good.' Giving her a lopsided smile, Dylan stared around him, obviously thinking. 'Let's start with the bedrooms.'

'The suites? Or the luxury doubles?' Which would be best? He'd already seen the best suite in the place—he was staying in it. So maybe the doubles…

'The uninhabitable ones,' Dylan said, cutting short any hopes of impressing him that morning. Sadie silently cursed her loose tongue over dinner. It had to be the fault of the wine.

'Right this way,' she said, her smile fading the moment she turned away to press the 'Call Lift' button.

The bedrooms were worse than she remembered. A lot worse.

'Lot of work needed here,' Dylan said, winning the prize for understatement of the year. Sadie sighed as she took in the broken tiles, missing bed, ripped wallpaper and strange black marks on the carpetless floor.

'Yes,' she agreed. 'And a lot of money to do it.' If there were anything guaranteed to send Dylan running…and she'd brought him straight there. Why had she even given him the choice?

But Dylan just shrugged and smiled. 'But I've seen worse. Okay. Now let's see the ones you've done up.'

Sadie wanted to ask what sort of hotels he'd been staying in, to have seen worse, but instead she decided to grab the life belt with both hands and swim for the shore. 'Luxury doubles coming up,' she said, with a smile that made her face ache.

At least she knew they had carpets.

By the time they were done viewing the hotel, Sadie was exhausted from excessive smiling and from scraping around in her brain for the answers to Dylan's incredibly detailed questions. At least she could never complain that he wasn't taking this business proposal seriously. For all his tourist clothes, he'd been professional to the hilt, asking questions she'd never even imagined she'd need to know the answers to.

Back in the lobby, she looked over her scribbled list of things to look up for him. It was up to two pages already, and he'd only been there less than a day.

'I'd better get back to the office and type up my notes from this morning,' she said. 'I should have answers for you by this evening…'

'Oh, I'm not done with my tour yet, Mrs Sullivan.' He flashed a smile. 'I want to see the town next.' He looked her up and down, and Sadie resisted the urge to hide behind her clipboard. 'Why don't you go and get changed into something more suitable for sightseeing?'

Something more suitable… What had happened to this being all business? What was he imagining—a Hawaiian shirt and a bumbag? But she had said he was in charge, so she bit her tongue. Hard. 'Give me ten minutes.'

He nodded, but since he was already frowning at the screen of his phone she wasn't sure he noticed her leave.

As she dashed up to her room she ran through the morning again in her head. Dylan had seemed somewhat underwhelmed by the hotel as a whole, with far more questions than praise, but Kuşadasi was bound to impress. The local economy and the blossoming tourist trade was what made the Azure a safe bet. She just had to make sure he saw that.

Dylan was so like Adem, in so many ways, she thought as she slipped into a light sundress. Adem had always worked on gut instinct, trusting his feelings to lead him to the right decisions. And instinct mattered to Dylan too—so that was what she needed to win over.

Hadn't he made it clear his business specialised in short-term, in-and-out projects? All she needed to do was hold his attention long enough to get him to invest. Then the Azure would take off, she'd be able to pay him back or buy him out in no time, and it would be back to just her and Finn again.

Grabbing her sunglasses and bag, Sadie took a deep breath and headed down to wow Dylan Jacobs. Whether he liked it or not.

CHAPTER FOUR

IT ALMOST FELT like a date, Dylan thought as they sped down the Turkish roads towards the town centre. The Azure Hotel wasn't quite close enough to walk in—another point against it—but with Sadie sitting beside him in a pale cotton sundress, her dark hair loose to her shoulders, he found it hard to be objective.

Because this—being alone with her, exploring a new place, relaxing in her company—was everything he'd dreamed about once, in the secret places of his mind he'd never fully admit to. Back in the days when he'd let himself think about a world without his best friend, or one where he'd met Sadie first.

He hadn't let the fantasies into his mind often—he'd learned early in life there was no point wishing the world to be any different than it was unless you were willing to do something to change it. And he hadn't been willing, not in the slightest. If even imagining it had felt like betrayal, the idea of acting on those fantasies had been beyond contemplation.

Adem had been the right guy for Sadie—he'd always known that. Known he couldn't offer her half as much, so he'd never considered trying—not that he'd have risked or betrayed his friendships that way anyway. A woman like Sadie needed love, commitment—she deserved forever. And he didn't have that in him.

But now, with Sadie in the driver's seat, sunglasses on and legs bare under that sundress, he could feel those imagined possibilities rising again. And just for a moment he let himself believe that she wanted him here—for more than just his money.

A light turned red and they pulled to a stop, the jerk breaking the moment, and reality sank back in. If this were a date he'd planned, he'd know where he was going. Sadie would be smiling at him, not looking tense and nervous and sad. The familiar guilt wouldn't be sitting in his chest—smaller than when Adem had been alive, sure, but still ever present.

Plus he'd probably be driving.

The lights changed again, and Sadie manoeuvred expertly past waiting cars and swung into a suddenly vacant parking spot by the marina that Dylan hadn't even noticed. He had plenty of experience driving abroad himself, but for once he was glad to be driven. It was nice to see Sadie so in control in this place.

'Come and look at the ocean,' she said, sliding out of her seat and into the sunshine. 'It'll give you a feel for the place.'

They stood by the railings together, staring out at the Aegean, and Dylan felt a comfortable warmth settle into his bones—one he wasn't sure was entirely due to the sunshine. He was enjoying Sadie's company just a little too much. He'd always found her presence relaxing, to a point, but before he'd never allowed himself to indulge in that feeling too much. Here and now, though, it felt all too natural.

He shut his eyes against the sparkle of the sun on the

water. Business. That was what he was here for, and that was what he needed to concentrate on. He couldn't afford to forget himself here—he needed to keep on top of his other projects while he was away, as well as work on the Azure proposal with Sadie. Already that morning he'd had enough emails from his assistant back in Sydney to remind him that things never worked quite as smoothly when he was away. He had to stay on top of everything.

Eyes open again, he shut his mind to the view and the warmth of the sun, and turned his attention instead to the practical aspects of the place. A marina, filled with top-end private yachts—and further up, cruise ships. Suddenly he understood exactly why Sadie had parked where she had.

'So, this is your subtle way of telling me that Kuşadasi is a popular cruise-ship destination?' he said, turning his back on the marina to lean against the railing and study her instead.

She gave him a perfectly innocent smile. 'Pure coincidence, I assure you. But as it happens, yes, it is! Tourism is the heart blood of this place. The ships stop here regularly, filled with people ready to explore the town—and spend their money on souvenirs.'

Which all sounded good until you studied the logic behind it. 'But how many of them make it up the hill to the Azure?'

'That's not the point.'

'Of course it is. If the bulk of the tourists visiting this place are only here for the day, what do they need with a hotel?' She winced at his words, but recovered quickly. He had to admire her tenacity, even if her argument was weak.

'The cruise ships are only a small part of the tourist industry here—and, actually, they're the gateway to a whole new market. Some of the people who visit for a day might never have even considered Turkey as a holiday destination before—but after a few hours here they may well decide to come back for a longer stay. Or to tell their friends that it was a great place to visit. Or even look into buying holiday apartments or hotel time shares here.'

A slim possibility. People who liked cruises—like his mother and her third husband—tended to take more cruises, in Dylan's experience. But who knew? Maybe she was right. He'd need more figures before he could make a value judgement.

'Okay, then,' Dylan said, pushing away from the railings. 'So what is it about this town that will make them come back?'

'The history,' Sadie replied promptly. 'The shopping. The atmosphere. The food. The views. Everything.'

'So show me everything.'

'That could take a while.'

Dylan shrugged. 'We've got all day. So, what's next?'

Sadie looked around her then nodded to herself. 'Let's take a walk.'

That date-like feeling returned as they walked along the seafront towards a small island, linked to the mainland by a walkway. Dylan resisted the urge to take her arm or hold her hand, but the fact it even needed to be resisted unsettled him. Not just because this was *Sadie* but because he'd never really thought of himself as a hand-holding-in-the-sunshine kind of guy. He tended to work better after dark.

Sadie turned and led him along the walkway leading out into the sea towards the island, and Dylan distracted himself by reading the signs of fishing tours on offer and checking out the tourist trap stalls set up along the way, selling bracelets and temporary tattoos.

'What is this place?' he asked, nodding to the island up ahead. Covered with trees, it appeared to have a fortified wall running around it and plenty of people wandering the path along the edge of the island.

'Pigeon Island,' Sadie replied promptly. 'You see over there, above the trees? That's the fortress of Kuşadasi—built in the thirteenth century. It was there to protect the Ottoman Empire from pirates—including Barbarossa himself.'

'I didn't realise I was here for a history lesson, as well as a tourism one.'

'There's a lot of history here,' Sadie pointed out. 'And a lot of tourism to be had from history. Wait until you see the *caravanserai*.'

'I look forward to it.' History wasn't really his thing, but Sadie seemed so excited about taking him there he was hardly going to mention it. Maybe it would be more interesting than he thought, looking back instead of forward for once.

'There's a seafood restaurant and café and stuff inside,' Sadie said, as they reached the path around the island, 'although I thought we'd head back into town for lunch. But I wanted you to see this first.'

She stopped, staring back the way they had come, and Dylan found himself copying her. He had to admit, Kuşadasi from this angle was quite a sight, with its busy harbour and seafront. He could see what Adem had loved about the place.

'Does Turkey feel like home now?' he asked, watching Sadie as she soaked up the view.

She turned to him, surprised eyebrows raised. 'I suppose. I mean, we've been here for a few years now. We're pretty settled. I can get by with the language—although Finn's better at it than me.'

'That's not the same as home.' At least, from what little Dylan knew about it.

'Well, no. But, then, I never really expected that *anywhere* would be home again after Adem.'

One quiet admission, and the whole mood changed. He was wrong, Dylan realised, and had been all along. This was nothing like a date at all.

He looked away, down at the water, and tried to imagine what kept her there in Kuşadasi. It couldn't just be history and sheer stubbornness, could it? Especially given how strange and lonely it must be for her there every day in Adem's place, without him beside her.

She shook off the mood, her hair swinging from side to side as she did so, and smiled up at him. 'What about you? Where's home for you these days? Neal says you're operating mostly out of Sydney?' Changing the subject. Smart woman.

'Mostly, yeah. My mum left Britain and moved back home to Australia when she remarried again, and my sister is out there too now, so it makes sense.' And this time, finally, he had faith that they might both stay there now they'd each found some happiness in their lives. He felt lighter, just knowing they were settled.

'Do you see them often?' Sadie asked.

Dylan shrugged. 'It's a big country. We catch up now and then.'

'Between business trips.' Was that accusation in her tone? Because he wasn't going to feel bad for running a successful business, even if it meant always being ready to jump at a new opportunity and run with it—often in the opposite direction from his family.

'Pretty much. Between the office in Sydney and the one in London, I probably spend more time in the air than in my apartments in either city.'

He'd meant it as a joke, but even as the words came out he realised he'd never thought of it like that before. All those years trying to get his family settled, and he'd never stopped to notice that he didn't have the same grounding at all. He'd just assumed his business—solid, profitable and reliable—was enough to give that security. But in truth he was no more settled than Sadie was, in this country she'd never chosen for herself.

Maybe they were both drifting.

'We're both very lucky to live in such beautiful places, though,' Sadie said.

He tried to return her smile. 'Yes, I suppose we are. So, why don't you show me some more of the beauty of this place?'

'Okay.' She stepped away, back towards the promenade to the mainland. 'Let's go and take in the town.'

Home.

Sadie considered Dylan's question again as she led him into the town of Kuşadasi proper. She took him by the longer back route to give him a true feel for the place. In comfortable silence they walked through narrow cobbled streets filled with shops. Half their wares were hung outside—brightly coloured belly-dancing costumes and leather slippers butting up against shops selling highly patterned rugs, or with rails of scarves and baskets of soaps on tables in the street. The smell of cooking meat and other dishes filled the air as the local restaurants prepared for lunch, the scent familiar and warming to Sadie.

As they walked she could see Dylan taking everything in—reaching out to run his fingers over the walls, his eyes darting from one shop display to the next. Had she been so fascinated when she'd first visited? It seemed so long ago she could barely remember.

Would this place ever truly be home? Could it? Or would it always just be the place where she'd lost the love of her life?

When she thought of home she thought of her family—and so, by default, of the pretty English village where she'd grown up, just outside Oxford. She remembered playing in the woods with her sister Rachel, or taking walks on the weekend with their parents and stopping for lunch in a country pub. And she thought of later meeting Adem and his friends in Oxford, when she'd travelled in every day for her first proper job after training in a small, independent spa and beauty salon there. She thought of the first flat she and Adem had rented together in London, after they'd been married.

She didn't think of the Azure. Not because she didn't love it but because it seemed so alien to all those other things. Like a permanent working holiday.

She loved Turkey, Kuşadasi, the Azure. And maybe Dylan was right in an odd, roundabout way. If she wanted to stay there, she needed to find a way to make it feel like home.

They emerged from a side passage out onto the bigger main street, with larger stores and the occasional street vendor stall. Here, after the charm of the old town streets, Kuşadasi looked more modern, ready to compete in the world tourist market. It was important to show Dylan that they had both here.

Suddenly, Dylan stopped walking. 'Hang on a minute.' Turning, he walked back a few paces to a stall they'd just passed. Curious, Sadie followed—not close enough to hear his conversation with the stallholder but near enough to see what had caught his attention.

She rolled her eyes. A sign advertising 'Genuine Fake Watches'. Of course. In some ways Dylan really was just like Adem—they had the same absurd sense of humour and the same reluctance to let a joke lie untold.

Still, she smiled to see that Dylan wasn't pointing out the error to the stallholder, and instead seemed to be striking up a friendly conversation with him as he took a photo on his phone and examined the watches. Another way he was like her husband, she supposed—that same easy nature that made him friends everywhere he went. She'd never had that, really, and couldn't help but envy it.

'Enjoying yourself?' she asked, as he returned.

Dylan grinned. 'Immensely. What's next?'

She'd planned to take him to the *caravanserai*—she just knew his magpie mind would love all the tiny shops and stalls there, too, and it was a huge tourist attraction with plenty of history. But it was getting late and her stomach rumbled, nudging her towards the perfect way to remember why she was so lucky to live in Kuşadasi— her favourite restaurant.

'I think lunch,' she said, watching as Dylan slipped his own no doubt authentic and ridiculously expensive watch into his pocket and replaced it with the genuine fake he had just bought.

'Fantastic. I can show off my new toy.' He shook his wrist and, despite herself, Sadie laughed, feeling perfectly at home for the first time in years.

From the way Sadie was greeted at the door of the restaurant with a hug from an enthusiastic waitress, Dylan assumed she was something of a regular. Despite the queue of people ahead of them, they were led directly to a table right in the centre of the glass-roofed portion of the restaurant, with vines growing overhead to dull the power of the sun as it shone down.

He couldn't catch the entire conversation between

Sadie and the waitress, but he did notice it was conducted half in English, half in Turkish, with the waitress particularly shifting from one to the other with no sense of hesitation at all.

'Adem's second cousin,' Sadie explained. 'Or third. I forget. Most of the Turkish side of his family moved over to England at the same time his mum did, as a child, but one cousin or uncle stayed behind.' She handed him a menu. 'So, what do you fancy?'

'I get to order for myself today, then?' he teased, and she flashed him a smile, looking more comfortable than she had since they'd left the Azure that morning.

'I think I can trust you not to choose the burger and chips. But if you're fishing for a recommendation...'

'No, no. I think I can manage to choose my own food, thanks.'

She shrugged. 'Sorry. I think it's the mother thing. Finn always wants to debate all the options on the children's menu before he makes his choice.'

The mother thing. It still felt weird, identifying Sadie as a mother. Maybe because he'd spent far more time with her before Finn's birth than since. Just another reminder that she was a different woman now from the one he'd fallen so hard for in Oxford all those years before.

'So, what do you fancy?' she asked, folding her own menu and putting it to one side. Dylan got the feeling she had it memorised.

'The sea bass, I think.' He put his own menu down and within seconds their waitress was back to take their orders.

'Can I have the chicken salad today, please?' Sadie asked, smiling up at her friend. 'With extra flatbread on the side.'

'Of course. And for you, sir?'

As he looked up Dylan spotted the specials board behind the waitress. 'Actually, I think I'll have the lamb *kofta* off the specials, please.'

Sadie frowned at him as the waitress disappeared with their menus. 'I thought you wanted sea bass?'

He shrugged. 'Something better came along.'

She didn't look convinced, but rather than press the point she pulled a notepad from her bag and opened it to a clean page. Apparently they were back to business.

'So, while we have a quiet moment—what do you think so far?'

'Of Kuşadasi? It's charming,' he said.

'Not just the town.' Frustration creased a small line between Sadie's eyebrows. Despite himself, Dylan found it unbearably cute. 'Of everything. The tourist potential here, my plans for the hotel…the whole lot. Consider it a mid-visit review.'

'I've only been here less than a day,' Dylan pointed out.

'Really? It seems longer.' She flashed him a smile to show it was a joke, but Dylan suspected she meant it. After all, he was feeling it too—that feeling that he'd been there forever. That they'd never been apart in the first place.

A very dangerous feeling, that. Maybe Sadie was right. It was time to focus on business again.

Leaning back in his chair, he considered how to put his comments in a way that she might actually listen to rather than get annoyed by.

'Your plans…they're the same ones Adem mapped out when you moved here, right? And that was, what? Three years ago?'

She nodded. 'About that, yes. And, yes, they're his plans. He put a lot of time, energy and research into developing them. I was lucky. When he… When it all fell to me, I already had a blueprint to follow right there. I don't know if I'd have managed otherwise.'

'I think you would have done.' In fact, he rather thought she might have to. 'The thing is…are you sure that sticking to Adem's plans is the wisest idea?'

Her shoulders stiffened, and Dylan muffled a sigh. He should have known there wasn't a way to broach this subject without causing offence.

'You knew Adem as well as I did, almost anyway,' she said. 'Do you really think he wouldn't have triple-checked those plans before putting them into action?'

'Not at all.' In fact, he was pretty sure that Adem would have taken outside counsel, considered all the possibilities, and covered every single base before he'd committed to the Azure at all. Despite his enthusiastic nature and tendency to jump at opportunities, Adem had always been thorough. 'But what I mean is, the best plans need to be flexible. Adem knew that. Things change in business all the time—and quickly. Three years is a long time. The world economy, the tourist trade, even this place, aren't the same as they were then. That's why you need to review plans regularly and adjust course where necessary.'

'I thought you were here to provide investment, not business advice.' Her words came out stiffer than her frame.

Time to put his cards on the table. 'Sadie, I'm here to provide whatever it is you need—to survive here, to save your hotel, or just to be happy. But you have to trust me in order to get it.'

CHAPTER FIVE

TRUST HIM. WHAT A strange concept.

In the years since Adem had died Sadie had grown very good at relying on and trusting nobody but herself. After all, who else could she trust to care as much about Finn and the future of the Azure? Neal had helped, of course, but he'd always deferred to Adem's plan.

She should have known it wouldn't be as simple with Dylan.

Their food arrived and she picked at her salad and flatbread, loving the crunch against the soft gooeyness of the freshly baked bread. Eventually, though, she had to admit that she couldn't hide her silence behind food forever—and Dylan was clearly waiting for her to talk first. Either that or whatever information kept flashing up on his phone really was more interesting than lunch with her.

Actually, that was probably it. Still, she had to try and keep his attention.

With a sigh, she put the piece of bread she'd just torn down on her side plate.

'Look, I know what you mean—about the market changing, and all that.' Dylan looked up as she started to speak. She'd caught him just as he forked another mouthful of lamb between his lips, so at least she knew he wouldn't interrupt her for a moment or two. 'But sometimes you have to stick with a plan for a while to see its full potential. You have to give it time to work.'

There was silence again for a moment while Dylan chewed. Then he said, 'What if you don't have that kind of time?'

And wasn't that the nightmare scenario that kept her awake at night? But it was also why he was supposed to be here—to buy her the time she needed to make things work. He just had to give her that chance.

'You know, just because you're always chasing after the next big thing, that doesn't mean it's always the right thing to do.' Frustration leaked out in her tone. 'Jumping at every new trend or idea would just make us look unsteady and inconsistent. Some people like someone who can see things through—like Adem would have done with this plan. He'd have given it a chance to succeed, I know he would.'

Dylan winced at her words and Sadie realised that her comments could possibly be construed as more of a personal attack than a professional one. But it was too late to take them back now.

'Okay, I admit Adem was always better at committing than I was,' Dylan said. 'To a plan, or anything else for that matter. But he always knew when changes needed to be made, too. That's what made him such a good businessman.'

The most frustrating part was that he was probably right. In this one area Dylan had known Adem better than she could have—they'd worked together straight out of university, until Dylan had left to start his own business abroad, and Adem, newly married and planning a family, had declined to join him after a long talk with her. But until then they'd been the company's dream team, working completely in sync. Dylan was the one person in the world who truly knew what Adem would have done in her situation, and that irritated her.

'So what? You're going to give me a list of changes for the Azure and just enough pocket money to do them, then disappear for six months and let me get on with it?' she asked. 'But what happens next? I bet I can guess. You come back and move the goalposts again—because the market's changed or whatever—and give me a whole new list of changes.' She shook her head. She wouldn't do it. 'I can't work that way, Dylan. I can't *live* that way either. It's not fair to ask me to.'

'I never would,' Dylan shot back. His fork lay forgotten on his plate now, and the intensity in his gaze as he leant across the table was almost intimidating. 'That's not what I'm saying at all. All I mean is...let's go through Adem's plans together, see what needs tweaking or updating. I'm not throwing the baby out with the bathwater here, Sadie. I'm certain that Adem's plans are solid—or were three years ago. But just because you've made one plan doesn't mean you can't adapt or improve it when a better idea comes along.'

'Like switching from sea bass to lamb.' He made it all sound so simple and sensible.

Dylan smiled, relief spreading out across his face. 'Something like that.'

'Okay. I'll think about it.' And that was all the commitment she planned to make to this man.

'That's all I ask.'

They finished eating in silence. Sadie settled up the bill and they were back out on the street before Dylan asked where they were going next.

'The *caravanserai*,' Sadie said, with a faint smile.

'Another tourist site with a lot of history. I think you'll like this one.'

'I'm sure I will.'

The *caravanserai*, a fortified marketplace dating back to the seventeenth century, loomed up above them, its crenellations making it look more like a castle than a shopping centre.

'So, what is this place?' Dylan asked, squinting up at the tall walls.

'These days, part marketplace, part hotel and entertainment venue.' Sadie strolled through the marble arch, the splash of the fountains and the greenery surrounding the inner courtyard helping her relax, just like they always did. 'But back in the day it was a protected place for merchants and such passing through the town—they could be sure they and their merchandise would be safe behind these walls.'

'So I can see.' Dylan placed a hand against the stone wall. 'Solid.'

'Come on. Come and look at some local wares.'

There were fewer goods on offer now that the *caravanserai* was mainly a hotel, but Sadie suspected Dylan would enjoy what there was. She gave him a quick tour of the ground floor, slipping through stone archways into shady stores hung with rugs and other fabrics. Once she was sure he had his bearings, she left him examining some beautifully painted bowls and pottery and escaped back out to the courtyard and the refreshing sound of the falling water from the white fountain in the centre.

She needed a moment to think, a moment alone, without Dylan's presence scrambling her senses. She wasn't sure if it was because she associated him so closely with Adem, or because it felt at once so strange and yet so

natural to have him there in Turkey with her, but either
way it confused her. She couldn't think straight when he
was smiling at her, talking apparent sense that only her
personal knowledge of his history and her gut instinct
could counter.

She settled down to sit on the edge of the fountain,
letting the coolness of the marble sooth her palms, and
circled her neck a few times to try and relieve the tension that had spread there over lunch.

Of course, it was possible she'd only grown so de-
fensive with him because he'd been criticising Adem's
plan—because it had felt like betraying the man himself,
even if she knew intellectually Adem would never have
seen it that way. But Adem's plan was the only thing she
had left to tell her what her husband would have wanted
for her, for their son, and for their dream hotel.

In the absence of anything else she'd clung to it like
a life raft. Except it hadn't worked—and she had to face
the fact that, whatever Dylan said, that failure was more
on her than the plan. She had no doubt that if Adem had
been there, with all his charm and enthusiasm, he'd have
made it work—and they'd never have been in the position
of having to beg Dylan Jacobs for help at all.

If they needed a new plan, then she needed help. She
hadn't trained for this, hadn't ever planned to take it on.
She could run her spa business with military precision
and a profit every quarter—she knew what it needed and
what worked. But a whole hotel? She was lost. And she
was going to have to confess that to Dylan—not a conversation she relished.

But if she couldn't trust herself to come up with a plan
to save the Azure, could she really trust Dylan? Wasn't
he just another short-term sticking plaster? Oh, he meant
well, she was sure enough of that. But he didn't see things

through. Everyone knew that. Why would the Azure be any different for him?

Suddenly, a shadow appeared on the stone floor in front of her—dark and lengthening in the afternoon sun. Sadie looked up to see Dylan standing over her, a contrite expression on his face and a paper-wrapped parcel in his hands.

'For you,' he said, handing her the package.

'Why?' she asked, unwrapping the paper. 'I mean, thank you. But you shouldn't have.' The wrapping fell aside to reveal a beautiful silk scarf—one from the rack she'd shown him inside, but not one she'd ever have looked at for herself. Not because she didn't love it, or because it wouldn't suit her. The bright, vibrant colours were exactly the sort that her sister Rachel was always telling her she should wear, but she rarely did these days.

It was too bright, too bold for her. But, holding it, she wished more than anything she still had the guts to wear it.

'It's just a token,' Dylan said. 'An apology, I guess.'

Sadie shook her head, wrapping the scarf back up loosely in its paper. 'You don't have to apologise to me.'

'I feel like I do. I didn't mean to offend you, at lunch I mean.' He sighed and sat down beside her at the fountain. In an instant all the cool serenity Sadie usually found there vanished. 'You know I'd never badmouth Adem—you do know that, right? I know it's not the same as for you but…you know what he meant to me too.'

'I do.' Guilt trickled down inside her chest. Dylan and Adem had been best friends before she'd even met them. Miles might have separated them, but she knew Adem had stayed in close contact with both Neal and Dylan until the day he'd died. She didn't hold the monopoly on grief over his death.

'I'm not just doing this for him, though—helping you, I mean.' Dylan twisted to look her straight in the eye, and Sadie found it strangely difficult to look away. What was it about this man that was so captivating, so compelling? 'But you have to know I wouldn't give up on this—not on something that was so important to my best friend.'

'I know that,' Sadie said, but she knew it lacked the conviction of her previous agreement.

Yes, Dylan would want to do this for Adem. But she also knew that all he could really offer was a short-term solution at best. The money would keep them afloat, give them another chance, and his thoughts on the plans for the future of the hotel would be invaluable, she was sure. But it was going to take more than that to save the Azure. She needed to find a way to do that herself, once Dylan's money had been spent and the man himself had moved on. She couldn't rely on him to be there for anything more than cash and brief excitement at the start of a new project.

With a sigh Dylan reached across and took the scarf from her lap, unwrapping the paper again. Then, gently, he placed it around her throat, knotting it loosely at the front. The soft silk felt luxurious against her skin, and she couldn't help but smile at the bright pop of colours around her neck. Then she raised her chin, and her gaze crashed into his, heating her cheeks until she was sure she was bright pink. His fingers straightened the fabric of the scarf, brushing against her throat, and her skin tingled under his touch.

How long had it been since she'd felt a tingle like that? She could say exactly, to the day.

Not since her husband had died.

Sadie swallowed, hard, and shuffled back along her stone seat.

'I know I'm not Adem,' Dylan said, his voice softer now. 'And you know me, I don't do long term or commitment, not in my personal life. But if I say I'll take on a work project, I see it through to the end, whatever happens. You can trust me on that.'

Sadie nodded, knowing it was true as far as it went. But it wasn't the whole truth. 'Which is why you only ever take on short-term projects,' she pointed out, as gently as she could.

'Yeah. I suppose it is.' Dylan looked down at his hands, and a coolness spread across Sadie again now he wasn't staring at her.

He looked so forlorn that Sadie felt obliged to try and build him up again. After all, he *was* doing his best, and that had to be worth something. Besides, she needed him.

'Okay,' she said, 'we're in this together, then—if you can convince your stakeholders to invest.'

He glanced up again, a faint smile on his lips. 'I'll be as persuasive as I can with whatever proposal we come up with. So what's next?'

'I don't know about you, but I need some coffee.' She got to her feet, smoothing down the skirt of her sundress and adjusting the scarf. The bright colours looked just right against the pale dress somehow. 'Proper Turkish coffee.' She offered him a hand to pull him up.

'Sounds like just the tonic,' he replied, his fingers closing around hers.

Sadie hoped so. With the strange way she was feeling today she needed some sort of medicine. Or a slap upside the head.

Sadie chose a small coffee shop overlooking the marina. Dylan sat back and let her order while he took in the view. Still, the aroma of thick, burnt coffee beans took him back through the years—to epic coffee-fests with Adem and Neal at university, when they'd drink buckets of the stuff to get through revision or a particularly tough assignment. Or later, lounging around in Sadie and Adem's first flat in London, when they had all just been starting out—and burning the candle at both ends working full time and studying for MBAs or accountancy qualifications at night. They'd passed whole weekends just drinking coffee until it had been time to switch to beer.

'So,' Sadie said, as the waiter disappeared to fetch their coffee, 'you think I need to change direction with my plans.'

Yeah, he should have known that conversation wasn't over. The scarf apology seemed to have worked in the short term, but it didn't really change anything. Her plans were still stuck in the past.

'I think you need to consider new opportunities as they present themselves.' That sounded better, right? 'Adem always knew how to keep an eye out for a new opportunity—and when to jump at it.'

She pulled a face, her mouth twisting up into a grimace that would have been ugly on anyone else. Apparently his new approach didn't sound all that much better after all. 'I suppose you taught him that.'

Dylan frowned. What, exactly, was that supposed to mean? Stupid to pretend he didn't know. And she was right—she'd seen him jump at the chance of new work, new women, new places, new everything too often not to be. Dylan Jacobs didn't stick at anything—except success. And even then he'd found a way to make it fit his own natural tendencies towards the short term.

His sister Cassie always claimed he was just making sure to run first—before he could be left or hurt. Dylan had never had the heart to tell her that he was more afraid of hurting than *being* hurt. He might be his father's son in many ways, but he had a better handle on his own failings. If he couldn't give forever—and he couldn't—it was better never to promise more than just for now.

It had worked so far, anyway.

Sadie was still waiting for an answer. 'Maybe. We both learnt a lot from working together.'

No response. The waiter returned, carrying two tiny cups of thick, black sludge and little sugar pellets to sweeten it. Dylan busied himself stirring some into his coffee while he tried to figure out what he'd said now.

And then, when it became clear he wasn't going to work it out alone, he asked, 'Okay, what did I say this time?'

Sadie looked up from twirling her spoon anti-clockwise in her coffee and shook her head. 'Nothing. Really.' She faked a smile—and Dylan had seen enough of her real ones to be sure this one was fake. 'But we're letting our history colour our business discussions again, don't you think?'

Were they? Not really, Dylan decided. Which meant that whatever discussion she was having with herself in her head probably was. God, he really wished he knew what she was thinking.

'That's kind of inevitable, don't you think?' he asked. 'We've known each other a long time, after all.'

'I've barely seen you in the last five years,' Sadie pointed out.

'Which only makes it worse. We've got a lot of catching up to do.' Instinctively, he reached out to place his hand on hers, where it rested beside her coffee cup. 'And, Sadie, just because we haven't seen each other, that doesn't mean we're not still friends. That we're not still connected.'

She had to feel it too, that connection, tying them together through the years, however far he strayed. Surely she did, otherwise, he was all on his own out on this limb. He might not be able to stay, but it felt like he'd never truly left her either.

Sadie pulled her hand away, and Dylan's heart sank an inch or two.

'What would you like to do for dinner tonight?' she asked, not looking at him. 'I could book a table for you somewhere in town, if you'd like.'

For you. Not us. Yeah, that wasn't going to work for him.

Clearly the history thing was still bothering her. But as much as she wanted this to be all business, the truth was he wouldn't be there at all if it wasn't for their past. So maybe they needed to address that history head-on so they could move forward. On to a new business relationship, even if that was all it could ever be. At least he'd be able to help her.

He just had to find a way to get her to open up and talk to him about those five years he'd missed. And maybe, just maybe, what had happened before then.

Unfortunately, Dylan only knew one way to get those kinds of results. It worked with most of his clients' stumbling blocks—and it had always, always worked with Adem. Like the night he'd shown up pale and troubled, ring box in hand, trying to pluck up the courage to propose to Sadie, even though they had been far too young. Dylan had applied his usual technique, talked it out, and convinced Adem to do it—ignoring any cracking of his own heart as he'd done so.

The method was foolproof. It had precedent. No reason at all to think it wouldn't work with Sadie, too.

He needed to get her drunk.

Dylan drained his coffee, trying not to wince at the still-bitter taste. 'Town sounds good. But don't bother booking anywhere. I think tonight you need to show me the Kuşadasi nightlife.'

CHAPTER SIX

THE SAME WARDROBE, the same clothes—still nothing to wear. Sadie sighed and dropped to sit on her bed and study the contents of her closet from afar. What was she supposed to wear for a night out on the town anyway? She wasn't sure she'd ever had one in Kuşadası—since they'd arrived she and Adem had always been too busy with the hotel. Tonight would be the blind leading the blind.

Except, of course, Dylan was probably the expert at wild nights out in towns and cities across the globe. If she was lucky, maybe she could wait until he inevitably started chatting up some blonde at the bar then slip away home without him even noticing. That would be good. Sort of.

But even that incredibly depressing plan still required her to get dressed.

Eventually she settled on her smartest pair of jeans, a black top that had enough drape at the front to look vaguely dressy, and a pair of heels. She'd just have to rely on the make-up and jewellery she'd picked out to do the rest.

Sadie checked her watch—she still had half an hour before she needed to meet Dylan. The calculation of the time difference between Turkey and England was so automatic these days it was barely seconds before she'd fired up the laptop ready to Skype Finn, glad to see that her parents' computer was already online.

Finn knew the sound of the Skype call well enough that Sadie wasn't surprised when the video picture resolved to show his cheeky face already there, ready to chat. His cheeks were red and his hair a little sweaty around the hairline, as if he'd been doing a lot of racing around. From the shouts and laughs in the background Sadie guessed that his cousins were visiting, too. Good. He had little enough interaction with other children in Turkey; she'd hate to think of him getting lonely over in England, too.

'Hi, Mum!' Finn waved excitedly across the internet. 'Wow! You look really pretty tonight.'

Guilt poured over her in a rush, threatening to wash away her carefully applied eyeliner and lipstick. 'Thanks, little man,' she said, the words coming out weak. She shouldn't be dressing up for Dylan, shouldn't let her son see her looking pretty for another man, even if he was only a friend. She should be with Finn, sorting their future.

That's what I'm doing, part of her brain argued back. She needed Dylan to save the Azure.

When had it all grown so complicated?

'Are you having fun with Grandma and Granddad?' she asked. 'What are you up to?'

'Lots. CJ and Phoebe are here with Auntie Rachel. We've been playing in the garden, and next we're going to build the biggest Lego fort in the world ever!' Finn's eyes brightened with excitement, and Sadie felt a wave of love rush over her, the way she always did when she saw him happy. Whatever else seemed crazy in her life at the moment, Finn at least was as wonderful, perfect and precious as always.

'Sounds fun.' She was just about to ask him something else when the sound of two high-pitched voices yelling Finn's name cut her off.

'Sorry, Mum. Gotta go. CJ needs me for the fort. Otherwise Phoebe will make it a pink princess castle again.' Finn's words came out in a rush as he moved further away from the screen. 'Bye, Mum!'

'Love you,' Sadie called after him, but all she could see was the back of his head, disappearing through the door to the other room. Well. Who was she to try and compete with a Lego fort, anyway?

Before she could end the call her sister Rachel appeared on the screen, settling into the chair Finn had just vacated. 'Sorry. They're just having so much fun together. It's lovely.'

'That's okay,' Sadie said with a smile. 'I'm just glad he's not missing me.'

'Liar.' Rachel grinned back. 'At least part of you wishes he was pining away without you. Go on, admit it.'

'Maybe a very small part.'

Rachel nodded. 'You wouldn't be human otherwise.' She squinted at the screen, and Sadie tried not to duck away under her sister's scrutiny. 'He's right, though. You *do* look pretty. What's going on there worth dolling up for?'

She groaned inwardly. She should have called *before* she'd got ready. She couldn't lie to Rachel—she'd tried often enough over the years, but her sister always saw through it. But how to tell the truth?

'I've got a potential investor visiting,' she said in the end. 'He wants to see the Kuşadasi nightlife. Does this look okay for bar-hopping? It's been so long I can't remember.'

'Stand up and give me a twirl,' Rachel instructed, and

Sadie did as she was told. 'It's perfect. So…this potential investor. Is he cute?'

Sadie sat back down with a bump. Cute wasn't exactly the word she'd use to describe Dylan. Heartstoppingly gorgeous but totally untouchable? Closer to the mark. Still, she wasn't saying that to Rachel.

'I suppose so,' she said, as neutrally as she could.

'And is there…dare I risk to hope it? Is there fizz?'

Fizz. The word they'd used as teenagers to describe that intangible connection, that feeling that you just had to touch that other person, be close to them, feel their smile on your face or you'd just bubble over and explode. Did Dylan have fizz? Silly question. He'd always had fizz. That was the problem. And when he'd placed that scarf around her neck and his fingers had brushed her skin…

'There *is* fizz!' Rachel announced gleefully. 'Don't try and deny it. I can tell these things. Psychic sister skills.'

Sadie shook her head. 'It doesn't matter if there is or isn't fizz. The investor…it's Dylan. You remember Adem's best man? He's just here because he wants to help out with the Azure, but he needs to convince his stakeholders we're a good investment so I'm trying to give him enough plus points to present a great proposal to them.'

'Dylan? Of course I remember Dylan. If I hadn't been already married at your wedding…'

'Then you could have lined up behind the other bridesmaids for a shot at him.'

'He was more than cute, Sadie,' Rachel pointed out. As if she hadn't noticed.

'He's an old friend.'

'So? There's fizz.'

'He's *Adem's* old friend,' Sadie stressed, hoping her

sister would just figure it out without her having to spell it out.

'Which means Adem trusted this guy,' Rachel countered. 'Which means you can too.'

'With my hotel, maybe. Not with any fizz.' Even if she *was* ready to throw herself back into romance with a one-night stand or something, Dylan Jacobs would not be a good choice. And if she was even *thinking* about anything longer term, he'd be the worst choice in the world. He'd said it himself, he didn't do commitment. And she couldn't be in the market for anything less. She had her son to think of.

But Rachel clearly didn't get that. 'Why not?'

'Rachel...'

Her sister sighed, the sound huffing across the computer speakers. 'It's been two years, Sadie. Adem wouldn't want you sitting out there all alone, you know that. He'd understand.'

'Maybe,' Sadie allowed. Her husband had been loving, generous and wonderful. He probably would want her to be happy again with someone else. On the other hand... 'But I'm sure he wouldn't want me with Dylan Jacobs either.' He'd want her settled and stable—not things on offer from Dylan, even if he was interested.

'Why on earth not?'

'He's not that sort of guy, Rach. Besides...' She trailed off, not wanting to put the thought into words.

'Now we're getting to it. Tell me.'

Sadie took a deep breath, and confessed. 'If I admit to feeling...fizz with Dylan now, isn't that the same as admitting I felt it when Adem was alive, too?'

'Oh, Sadie.' Sympathy oozed out of Rachel's words and expression. 'Fizz, attraction...it's just that. We all feel it from time to time, with all sorts of people. It's what we do with it that counts. Sometimes we ignore it, and sometimes we act on it and see what happens next.' She paused. 'You didn't, right? Act on it with Dylan, I mean, before?'

'No!' An easy truth. But it didn't stop the niggling guilt reminding her that she'd thought about it.

'Then don't beat yourself up about it. Go out with the guy tonight. Relax. Enjoy a little fizz...'

Sadie groaned. 'I'm going to pretend you're talking about prosecco.'

'Ha! Whatever helps you loosen up a bit.'

'I'd better go.' Sadie checked her watch to be sure. 'Tell Finn I love him. And that I'll call tomorrow.'

'Will do,' Rachel said with a nod. 'Now, go and have fun.'

With a weak smile Sadie clicked the 'end call' button. A whole evening watching Dylan flirt with barmaids and blondes. She had a feeling that fun was the last thing she should expect tonight to be. Maybe more some sort of weird torture technique devised purely to drive her insane.

'And yet I'm going anyway,' she murmured to herself as she gathered up her light jacket and handbag. 'The things I do for this hotel...'

Tipping his chair back against the wall behind him, Dylan watched Sadie's slim form as she made her way across the bar from the bathrooms, wondering if she'd notice he'd replenished their drinks in her absence. Operation Drunk Conversation was now officially two drinks in, and he still felt a little uneasy about it. Apparently Bar Street was the place to go and get drunk in Kuşadasi, although with its range of Irish and British bars, as well as some Turkish ones, Dylan wasn't sure this was necessarily the local colour he'd be trying to sell to the stakeholders. On the other hand, it clearly brought in plenty of tourists—and money. It almost reminded him of their student days.

She looked younger in jeans and heels, he decided. Almost like she had back in London as a twenty-something. She'd filled out a little since then, he supposed, but only in the best ways. Her slender curves enticed him as she swerved through the crowds to reach him. His head filled with music, the way it had the first time he'd ever met her—the Beatles' 'Sexy Sadie' playing on a loop through his mind.

'You're still alone. I'm amazed.' Sadie slipped into her seat and took a sip of her wine without commenting on the level in the glass.

'Why amazed?'

'Well, five minutes always used to be more than enough time for you to find a girl to flirt with when we used to go out.' There was no bitterness or censure in her voice, more amusement, but Dylan felt the words like paper cuts all the same. Probably because they were true.

'Times have changed.'

'Not that much,' Sadie said. 'Neal keeps me updated on your exploits, you know.'

He bit back a curse. But, on the other hand, she'd given him the in he'd been waiting for—the first reference to the good old days. 'I was just thinking how much younger you look in jeans, actually. Like you used to, back in London. I half expected Adem to appear and put his arm around you.'

Sadie's smile turned a little sad. 'Would that he could.'

'Yeah. It must be hard, being here without him. The memories, I mean.'

'We never came here, actually,' Sadie said, looking

around her curiously at the crowded bar. 'But you meant Turkey itself. The Azure.'

'I did, yeah,' Dylan agreed. Dare he push it yet? Just a little? 'No one would have blamed you for selling up and leaving, you know.' He needed to understand why she hadn't. What made her commitment to this place so strong? What was it about Sadie that made her so able to commit and stick? And what was missing in him?

'It wouldn't make any difference where we were anyway,' Sadie said, which didn't answer the question he hadn't asked, but Dylan supposed he couldn't really blame her for that. 'I see Adem every day when I look at Finn—and, to be honest, I love that reminder.'

Of course she did. He'd never seen any couple as in love as Adem and Sadie. He didn't really need her to answer—he knew. The Azure was her way of holding onto the love of her life. Just because he'd never felt like that about someone didn't mean he couldn't see it in others.

'I'm glad you have that.' The truth, even if it carried a little pain with it. 'I'm sorry. I should have visited more. Spent more time with Finn.'

'Yes, you should,' she said, mock-sternly. 'Why didn't you?'

Did she really not know why? After that night at Kim and Logan's wedding he'd been sure his motives for staying away had been more than clear—and that she'd be grateful he had. Unless she didn't remember? She *had* been pretty drunk. So had he, of course, or it never, ever would have happened in the first place.

Misgivings began to creep up on him when he thought again about his plan. The two of them, drunk alone together, hadn't ended well in the past. But he didn't know another way to get her to loosen up around him.

'Work, mostly,' he lied, realising she was still waiting

for an answer. 'But I'm ready to fix that now.' He raised his glass. 'To absent friends.'

'Absent friends,' Sadie echoed. Lifting her own glass, she drank deeply, unconsciously giving him exactly what he wanted. It was too late for misgivings now anyway. It was time to put the plan into action.

'Hey, do you remember the time Neal got locked out of that hotel wearing nothing but a corset and stockings?'

Sadie burst into laughter, putting her glass down too hard on the table so wine sloshed over the edge. 'Of course I do—it was my corset! What I don't remember is how he persuaded me to lend it to him.'

'You've always been a soft touch for Neal,' Dylan said. 'Besides, he had a very good story. I should know, I made it up.'

She slapped his arm. 'You deviant. Tell me the whole story, then—the truth this time.'

It was going to work, Dylan could tell. By morning they'd have exorcised all their ghosts and memories and be able to move on. To be the friends and business partners Sadie needed them to be.

And nothing more.

He took a glug of his beer and started the story.

'Well, there was this girl, see…'

Several bars later Sadie could feel the alcohol starting to get to her—in that pleasant, slightly buzzy way that meant it was time to stop before another drink seemed like a really good idea. Otherwise tomorrow would be no fun at all. *Now* she remembered why she didn't do this any more.

'I need to call it a night.' She pushed her still half-full glass across the table away from her.

'Not a bad idea.' Dylan drained the last of his pint. 'You always were the sensible one.'

'Somebody had to be.'

She gave him a friendly grin and he returned it, his smile all at once totally familiar and yet somehow new. It made that buzzy feeling in her limbs turn a little more liquid, like honey.

They'd talked all evening, almost without pause. She'd worried, when he'd suggested this night out, that it would be awkward, the conversation stilted. But instead they'd fallen into old patterns, chatting about the past in the way only friends who'd done their most significant growing up together could. The conversation had covered everything from the day they'd met until the last time they had all been together before Adem had died.

Everything except one night—the night of Kim and Logan's wedding.

Did he even remember? And, if so, how much? Curiosity was burning inside her with the need to know. Had *she* remembered wrong? It had been so long ago she was starting to doubt her own memories. They'd both been pretty drunk that night...

But she wasn't drunk tonight. Just tipsy enough to be a little daring.

'What's the plan for tomorrow?' Dylan asked, getting to his feet and grabbing his jacket. 'I've got a business call first thing, then I'm all yours for the day.'

Tomorrow. Had she even made a plan for tomorrow? 'I thought maybe the beach?'

'Lying prone in the sun sounds like the perfect way to deal with my inevitable hangover.' He groaned as they headed for the door. 'I am officially too old for this.'

Sadie smiled. 'I never thought I'd hear you admit to that.'

'We all have to grow up some time,' Dylan said with a shrug, and somehow it felt like he was saying far more than just the words.

Outside, the autumn evening air had turned a little chilly, and Sadie shivered as they walked along the seafront, looking out for an empty cab.

'Cold?' Dylan asked. Then, without waiting for an answer, he slung an arm around her shoulder for warmth. A friendly gesture, Sadie knew. That was all it was—and nothing he and Neal hadn't done often enough in the past. But suddenly, here and now, as the fabric of his jacket brushed her bare neck she felt it. Fizz. Undeniable, impossible to ignore, fizz.

It was no good; she needed to know. And she was just drunk enough to ask.

'I've never asked you. Do you remember Kim and Logan's wedding?'

Dylan squinted out towards the ocean. 'That was the one up in Scotland, right? Where we all stayed in that weird hotel down the road and kept the bar open all night.'

'And Adem and Neal got into a drinking competition and passed out on the sofas in the next room.'

'I remember,' Dylan said, and even the words sounded loaded. 'You and Adem had been together, what? About a year?'

'Something like that. Do you remember what you asked me that night?'

He was standing so close, his arm around her shoulders, that she could feel his muscles stiffen. Oh, yeah, he remembered. 'Do you? We never… You never mentioned it again, so I always figured you must have forgotten. We weren't exactly sober that night.'

She'd gone too far to back out now. 'You asked me if

I'd ever wondered what might have happened if I'd met you first instead of Adem.'

'Yeah.' He let out a long breath. 'You said you hadn't.'

'And I truly hadn't, until that moment.'

The words hung there between them, the implication both clear and terrifying. They'd stopped walking without Sadie even realising, and suddenly a taxi pulled up beside them, the driver rolling down the window to ask where they wanted to go.

'The Azure, please,' Sadie said, shuffling along the back seat to let Dylan in beside her.

They rode in silence for a long moment before Dylan asked, 'And after?'

'After?' She knew what he was asking, but she needed a moment before she answered.

'After that moment. Did you…?'

She looked away. 'I wondered.'

'Huh.' Dylan slumped back against the car seat, as if all the tension had flowed out of his body with her words. Then he shook his head, laughing a little—Sadie got the impression it was at himself, rather than her. 'And then, of course, I tried to kiss you like a total idiot and—'

'Wait. What? I don't remember that bit.' And surely, surely that was the part she *would* remember, however much she'd had to drink.

'Don't you?' Dylan smiled, the expression shaded in the darkness of the cab. 'It was after we'd lugged Adem and Neal up to our rooms. You gave me a hug goodnight and…' He shrugged, trailing off. 'You pushed me away, of course.'

'I can't believe I don't remember that.'

'I'm glad you didn't,' Dylan said. 'Not my finest hour. I felt absolutely awful the next day—and was very glad one of us had been sober enough to be sensible.'

Sadie turned away, searching her memory for the lost moment and coming up blank. How different might their world have been if she'd remembered the next day? If she'd confessed to Adem? A thousand different paths spiralled from that moment, all but one untaken. And she wouldn't want to change it, she realised, not really. She wouldn't give up the years she'd had with Adem, or having Finn, for anything in the world. Things had worked out exactly as they were supposed to.

But that didn't stop her imagining what it might have felt like. And, God, did that bring a bucketload of guilt with it, right there.

Before she'd had time to work her way through half her emotions, they were back at the Azure. She paid up in a daze and walked inside, heading for the lift with Dylan beside her.

'You okay?' he asked, as the doors opened.

She nodded, and stepped inside, pressing the button for her floor on autopilot. 'Fine. So, tomorrow. Meet you in the lobby at ten?'

'Perfect.' He leant across her to press the penthouse button as they started to move. 'Sadie—'

'Don't worry about it,' she said, too fast. 'It's all in the past now.'

The lift dinged as it reached her floor, and she stepped towards the doors before they were even open.

Suddenly there was a hand at her waist, spinning her round, and Dylan was closer than she'd imagined, so close she could feel the heat of him.

'I might be about to be an idiot again,' he said.

Sadie swallowed, her mouth too dry. God, she wanted it. Wanted to feel his lips on hers, to see what she'd missed all those years ago. But the guilt that filled her had sobered her up and was already moving her feet backwards as the lift doors opened.

'Goodnight, Dylan.' She pulled away, stepping out, watching the frustration and fear crossing his face as the doors closed behind him and the lift whisked him away.

CHAPTER SEVEN

DYLAN WOKE UP the next morning to the sound of his phone alarm buzzing, far too early, and his head throbbing in time with the beeps. As if he needed the physical reminder of last night's exploits to give him a bad feeling about the day ahead.

He fumbled for the phone and switched off the alarm, his poor, tired brain trying to catch up with the day. He had a conference call. He had to deal with Sadie. He really needed a shower.

Deciding that the last might help with the previous two items, he hauled himself out of bed and into the bathroom, thoughts flying at him as fast as the water from the wonderfully powerful showerhead.

If he was feeling bad this morning, chances were that Sadie was feeling worse. And not just physically. He knew her tendency to beat herself up about things that weren't her fault, or weren't even all that wrong in the first place, and he had a feeling this morning would be a doozy.

Still, as bad as he felt for making her life more difficult than it already was—or at least more morally and emotionally complicated—he couldn't help but smile, remembering that for the first time since he'd met her he knew he wasn't in this alone. Not completely.

Switching off the water, he dried, dressed and managed to make it through the conference call—hopefully without any obvious signs of his hangover or his preoccupation. As he hung up, scribbling a last few notes to himself for later, he checked the clock. Still twenty minutes before he was due to meet Sadie. Should he work, nap or...?

He picked up his phone and hit the familiar key combination to call Neal. Yeah, it was early in Britain, but Neal had always been an early bird anyway. Except after nights out with him and Adem.

'How's it going?' Neal asked, in lieu of an actual greeting. 'You signed over your life savings to her yet?'

If he thought that would work... 'Nah. I got her drunk and told her the whole story about you and her corset instead.'

'Cheers. I'll look forward to that coming up next time we have a business meeting,' Neal said. 'But, seriously, how is she?'

'Probably hungover but otherwise fine.' He hoped.

Neal sighed. 'What did you do?'

'Nothing.' Much.

She'd try and pull back now, he could feel it. Try and put that distance they'd crossed last night back between them. Unless he could convince her not to.

'Although...' Dylan said, and Neal groaned.

'Here we go. Tell me.'

'I might have questioned Adem's plan for the Azure a bit. It needs updating.'

'So what? You're going to stay in Turkey and develop a better one?' Neal sounded sceptical.

'I'm going to work with her to develop one before I leave,' Dylan corrected him. She didn't have time to pull back. He only had a few more days to help her; they had to keep working. She'd see that, right?

Maybe the best thing was for them both to pretend that last night had never happened, just like last time. At least, once the headache faded.

'Are you, now?' Dylan didn't like the sudden raised interest level in Neal's voice.

'I am. What about it?'

'Just sounds like more involvement than you'd planned on,' Neal said. 'A lot more.'

Since Dylan's original plan had been get in, get out, send Sadie cash afterwards and never have to think about the Azure again, Neal had a point. He hadn't wanted to torment himself more than necessary by staying in her presence when she was more available than ever but still every bit as untouchable.

But all that had changed with two words. *I wondered.*

'She needs more help than I expected,' Dylan said, hoping his friend would accept the excuse.

'She needs every bit of help she can get,' Neal agreed with a sigh. 'I'm glad you're there.'

'So am I.'

Yes, he was still leaving in three days. And, yes, he knew he'd never be Adem, never be the love of Sadie's life. He wasn't imagining some perfect golden future for them together or anything.

But just knowing that she'd thought about it—about them—too? Well, that gave him hope.

And sometimes that was all a guy needed to get through the day.

The first thing Sadie registered when she woke up was her dry mouth. Next came the crushing weight of what felt like a boulder on her chest.

Last night had been everything she'd planned to avoid. How was she supposed to go back to All-Business Sadie after admitting that she'd imagined them together? And for the last twelve years…

After learning he'd tried to kiss her, too.

After almost letting him kiss her last night.

She pulled the pillow over her head and hoped it muffled her agonised groan.

And now she had to spend a whole day on the beach with him. In swimwear.

It all just went to prove that there really *was* a special hell for women who ogled their husband's best friend.

Escaping from her pillowy cage, she took deep breaths and tried to let the morning air soothe her—and her hangover. She needed to be calm and reasonable about this. As she had been about everything else she'd dealt with since Adem had died. She—and the Azure—needed Dylan. They needed his money, his investment and, much as she hated to admit it, his business brain, too. So she needed to find a way to make this right.

And, hopefully, considerably less awkward.

As she kicked off the covers and contemplated, Rachel's words from the night before floated back through her distracted brain. In some ways her sister had been right—as usual. Adem wouldn't want her to be alone or lonely. Which wasn't to say he'd want her to be rushing into the arms of another man either, but Sadie knew he wouldn't expect her to be alone forever.

She had, though. For the last two years the very idea of being with someone else had felt completely alien, the sort of thing that could only happen to other people. Adem had been the love of her life. Where was there to go from there really?

But last night, for the first time, the idea of moving on had seemed like a possibility. The thought of kissing another man had, for once, not filled her with revulsion or even confusion.

She'd wanted to kiss Dylan. And that was absolutely terrifying.

Because even if she was ready to *maybe* think about *possibly* moving on and *perhaps* just *thinking* about dating again, Dylan Jacobs was not the man to move on with.

If she had been after a fling or a one-night stand, something to get her back in the dating game, then maybe. But she wasn't a one-night stand sort of girl, never had been. And now…she had responsibilities. Commitments that had to come before a little personal pleasure.

She had Finn.

She wouldn't be another notch on Dylan's bedpost—and with a guy like Dylan she knew that was all she could ever be.

No, last night had taught her something far more important than the fact he'd tried to kiss her once. It had taught her that they still had history, and friendship, even with Adem gone. Sadie wanted Dylan to stay part of her life—and part of Finn's. She wanted her son to learn about his father from the people who had loved him most—and that had to include Dylan.

Another reason, if she'd needed one, why she couldn't risk anything more with him. She knew him, too well perhaps. One night in his bed and he'd hit the road, not coming back until he was good and certain that she wasn't getting any ideas about things between them going anywhere.

Better to keep things simple. Maybe they couldn't be just business—but they could definitely be just friends.

Now she just needed a way to get that across to Dylan.

Lying back against her cool sheets with the covers off,

she let the breeze from the open window caress her skin as she considered her options. This wasn't a conversation she wanted to have with him while she was wearing a bikini. She needed to stall a little before they got to the beach. Then he could sunbathe, nap, explore, ignore her the rest of the day, whatever he wanted. As long as he understood how things were going to be.

Sadie smiled to herself as the perfect solution presented itself. And it might just solve both of their hangovers, too.

It was hard to tell what Sadie was thinking or feeling when Dylan met her in the lobby. Her eyes were hidden behind oversized dark glasses, her hair pulled back from her face, and she wore a light skirt and tee shirt. From the large straw bag she carried, with towels peeking out the top and a bottle of suntan lotion in the front pocket, he assumed they were still on for the beach. Beyond that, he had no idea how the day might play out—and she didn't seem inclined to tell him.

'Ready to go?' she asked, the moment he approached. When he nodded, she spun on her heel and headed out, slipping behind the wheel of her car and waiting for him to join her.

They drove in silence for about ten minutes, while Dylan thought up a dozen conversation starters in his head. But every time he turned to use one of them Sadie's cool indifference to his presence stopped him.

He had to let her go first.

The first rumblings of doubt started in his mind when Sadie pulled in at a tumbledown farmhouse on the side of the road. There was no sign of anyone else around, but she jumped out of the car all the same and waited for him to follow.

A terrace sat outside the house itself, covered with vines and greenery, right next to the road. Sadie climbed the rickety wooden steps up to it and, after a moment, Dylan did the same.

'Um, did we add something to today's itinerary?' he asked, as they stood alone on the terrace.

'Trust me,' Sadie replied. 'We need this.'

What he really needed was a few more hours of sleep and some mega-painkillers, but she'd asked for his trust, so he'd give it to her.

After a moment the door to the farmhouse opened and a man walked out, smiling widely at Sadie, hands open in welcome. Sadie grinned back, and the two of them spoke in Turkish for a moment or two. Dylan didn't even try to guess what they were saying.

The man motioned to a nearby table, bare wood with benches to match, right at the edge of the terrace with a great view of the passing cars and the dusty fields beyond. But Sadie sat without question, so Dylan did the same.

'So this is…?' he asked.

Before Sadie could answer, a woman in an apron appeared, her dark hair coiled at the back of her head, and placed a strange metal pot, two glass teacups and a basket of bread on the table.

'Breakfast,' Sadie answered, reaching for the bread. 'Told you we needed it.'

Dylan started to relax. Maybe the woman had a point after all. He hadn't managed to make it down to the restaurant that morning, and his stomach definitely needed food.

The dishes kept coming, carried out by the man and the woman while Sadie explained about Turkish tea and waited for it to brew before pouring it. Dylan salivated at the sight of sweet, thick honey for the bread, bowls of olives, scrambled eggs with chorizo, chunks of salty feta cheese and a huge fruit platter. It might not be the full English he'd usually rely on to finish off a hangover, but Dylan had a feeling it would be more than up to the task.

They ate mostly in silence, Dylan savouring every mouthful of the delicious and obviously freshly cooked food. And as they ate, Dylan's hangover wasn't the only thing that started to recede. Somehow, without talking about it or even acknowledging it was there, the tension that had been pulled tight between them since they'd met in the lobby that morning started to loosen, just enough for him to relax.

The powers of good food truly were transformative.

As Sadie mopped up the last of the chorizo and eggs with the end of the bread, Dylan poured out the final dregs of the tea, knowing that things were about to change.

It was time for The Talk.

God, he hated The Talk.

Steeling himself, he waited for her to begin.

'Okay. So, I thought we needed that before we could deal with...' Sadie trailed off.

'Last night,' Dylan finished for her. No point beating around the bush now. 'Good call.'

Sadie picked up her paper napkin and began twisting it between her fingers. 'Here's the thing. I figure you wanted to go out last night to remind me that we're not just business. We have history.'

'I guess, a bit. Perhaps.' It hadn't been much of a plan, but it still discomfited Dylan a bit to have it seen through so easily.

'And you're right,' Sadie went on, apparently uncon-

cerned by his manipulations. 'I get it. We're friends—
and I don't want to lose that.'

'I'm glad to hear it.' Ah, so this was the way it was.
She was actually giving him the old 'I don't want to ruin
our friendship with sex' talk. He'd never been on this
side of it before.

It kind of sucked.

But her friendship mattered to him—no, just having
her in his life mattered to him. Any way that worked for
her. So he'd go along with it, despite the stinging pain
that had taken up residence in his chest. Because what
else did he have to offer her, really?

'I want you to be part of Finn's life.' She leant across
the table, shifting plates and bowls out of her way. Dylan
rescued the remains of the honey, which were perilously
close to her elbow. 'I want him to know about his dad
from the people who really knew and loved him—and
that includes you.'

She sounded so earnest, so determined that he couldn't
even find it in himself to be mad or frustrated. Because,
of course, it was all about Adem in the end. He should
never have imagined that it could be otherwise.

'But as for the rest of it,' Sadie said, sitting back again,
the distance between them yawning open, 'there's no
point dwelling on the past. Right?'

'I've always tried not to,' he said mildly. Tried not
to think about how different his life might have been if
his father hadn't walked out and left them, if he hadn't
spent his youth protecting his mother and sister, taking
care of them, finding the money for the household bills
each week. How different *he* might be. Life was what it
was—no point pretending otherwise.

Except, of course, that was exactly what he was doing
every time he thought about Sadie and imagined what

could have been, maybe. What they could have had if he'd been the one she'd run into with a full cup of coffee one rainy Oxford day instead of Adem.

Stupid, really. It wouldn't have made any difference. They'd have flirted perhaps. Maybe even dated for a bit. But if she thought he wasn't the settling-down sort now, it was nothing compared to how he'd been at twenty-one. He'd have sabotaged things within a month—and Sadie would probably have cried on Adem's shoulder, and they'd have fallen in love anyway.

Just the way it was supposed to be.

'I'm ready to face the future now, I think.' Bravery shone out of Sadie's face, and Dylan tried to shake away his melancholy thoughts and listen. 'I'm really ready to build a new future out here for me and my son—not just keep living Adem's dream and his plan.'

Did she really think that counted as moving on? She'd still be here, in the place Adem had chosen for them. She might think this was a big step forward, but to Dylan it still looked like clinging to the past.

The past was all well and good, but living there wasn't going to help Sadie find her spark again. For that, she needed to move on to her own dreams. And he was there to help her do that.

'So, what does that mean?' he asked.

'It means I'm ready to listen to your plans, instead of insisting on following Adem's,' Sadie said. 'You tell me what we need to do at the Azure, and we'll do it. What-ever it takes to save this place for Finn.'

For Finn. That was why she thought she was doing this. Interesting.

'Great.' It wasn't moving on, not really. But it might be the best he got from her, and at least it gave him a way to help her. It could be worse. 'Then let's get to the beach.'

'The beach?' Her nose crinkled up adorably, and Dylan looked away to stop himself staring at it.

'I always do my best brainstorming when I'm relaxing,' he said, faking a smile.

CHAPTER EIGHT

LADIES' BEACH WAS comfortingly familiar to Sadie. As they walked from the car down onto the soft sand she took deep breaths and let the salt air fill her lungs, while the sound of gulls and families playing in the sand and surf echoed in her ears. But even as she let the comfort of the seaside wash over her, the feeling that something was missing ached in her middle.

She missed Finn. He loved the beach so much—especially this one. They could play for hours, searching for shells to decorate sandcastles or jumping over the waves as they lapped against the shore. When they'd first moved here they'd spent almost every weekend at the beach the whole summer.

'It's a nice beach,' Dylan commented, his trainers dangling from his fingers as he walked barefoot beside her.

'Nice?' Sadie said disbelievingly. She took another look around her at the perfect yellow sand and bright blue water. 'It's perfect.'

Dylan chuckled. 'Okay, yeah. It's pretty gorgeous. I can see why this, at least, is a big draw for the tourists. Finn must love it here.'

'He does.' The heavy weight of a pebble of guilt joined the ache in her middle. When was the last time she'd brought Finn down to the beach? Things had just been so busy… 'We haven't made it down here together for a while, though.'

She flinched with surprise as Dylan's hand came up to rest against the small of her back, rubbing comfort through her tee shirt and steering her around a hole some enterprising young child had clearly spent some hours digging. She needed to pay more attention to where she was going. But Dylan's hand stayed at her back and the warmth of it, so much more heated than the bright sun overhead, was too much of a distraction in itself.

Friends, she reminded herself. That was what they'd agreed. And beyond one drunken attempt at a kiss she had no evidence at all he wanted anything more. A hand on the back was not seduction—however much it felt like it right now.

'When we get the Azure back on track, you'll be able to hire more help,' Dylan said, apparently oblivious to the effect his touch was having on her. 'Give you more time with Finn.'

'That would be perfect.' Finn deserved so much more than an overworked, stressed mother. She needed to be both parents to him now, and that meant being there all the time. A reduced workload would definitely help with that.

She just hoped it wouldn't be too reduced. After all, what else was she going to do once Finn was in bed or at school? And once Dylan was gone. All the times when she was alone again. She would need something to distract her then, and work was perfect.

Sadie almost laughed at herself. From one extreme to another—it seemed she'd always find something to worry about. They had to actually save the Azure first anyway, and that by no means felt like a sure thing.

Everything was so much harder without Adem there

to help—even if it was just someone else to help build sandcastles or explore seaweed clumps.

Suddenly Dylan stopped walking, right in the middle of an open patch of sand unmarred by castles or holes and a decent distance from any of the other beachgoers.

'This looks like the perfect spot,' he said, dropping his bag and towel to the sand.

'To brainstorm?' Sadie asked, one eyebrow raised.

He flashed her a smile. 'To sleep off the remains of my hangover.'

'I suppose that *is* the first step to saving my hotel,' Sadie said, only half sarcastically. After all, it was going to take Dylan on top form to help the Azure.

'Definitely.'

Without warning, he reached for the hem of his tee shirt and pulled it over his head, revealing more muscles and hair than she'd expected—and definitely more skin than she felt comfortable with as a friend. Sadie's mouth dried up and she swallowed painfully as she tried not to stare. God, but the man was gorgeous. She'd known that, of course, objectively. But she'd never spent much time with such upfront and undeniable proof, certainly not in the last decade.

Dylan had always been good looking, but now he'd grown into his looks completely. He wasn't a play*boy* any more, Sadie decided. He was all man.

She needed to get out of there. 'I'm going to go and swim.'

'Okay.' Dylan looked up from laying out his towel and grabbed for her wrist before she could turn away. His proximity and the feel of his skin on hers sent every sense she had into overdrive. How did anyone ever manage to be just friends with someone who looked like Dylan Jacobs? She needed some sort of handbook.

'Sadie,' he said, staring down into her eyes, his gaze so compelling she couldn't even think of looking away. 'I will find a way to save the Azure. You know that, right?'

Sadie swallowed again, her throat dry and raspy. 'I believe you.'

His mouth twisted up into a half-smile. 'Millions wouldn't, right?'

'This is business,' Sadie said with a shrug. Something she would do well to remember. 'And you know business. If anyone can save the Azure, it's you.'

'Only for you,' he murmured.

It was too much. 'Right. Swimming.' Sadie pulled her hand away from his and tugged down her skirt and pulled off her tee shirt, leaving her in just her sensible purple tankini. Then, with what she hoped was a friendly smile, she headed straight for the water.

She couldn't afford to be swayed by fizz, or touch, or the way he looked at her. Dylan looked at every woman he met that way, she was sure. He was a walking chemistry experiment for the female half of the human race. She couldn't read any more into that.

Money and business advice was all he had to offer her, and only for the short term. Once he got bored he'd be on the move again. She really needed to remember that.

Settling onto his towel, Dylan propped himself up on one elbow in the sand and watched Sadie's tankini-clad form sashaying towards the sea. He doubted she knew she was doing it, but her hips swayed as she walked all the same, her feet sinking into the sand. All those slender curves she kept so well hidden under dark suits and shapeless jackets were on display now and, friends or not, he wasn't going to miss a minute of watching them.

Friends. She'd sounded so certain over breakfast that friendship was all she wanted from him. After the night before, and her escape from the lift, he'd almost believed her. Until he'd touched her wrist on the beach and watched the colour flood her cheeks as their skin had met. Until he'd watched her watching him and known that whatever she thought she wanted, her body had other ideas.

Bad ideas, admittedly. She was a single mother with more responsibilities than money and a rigid sense of commitment that was in complete opposition to his own. But she wanted him. Maybe even half as much as he had always wanted her.

He couldn't give her what he knew she needed—what she'd always wanted since they'd met. Sadie was the kind of woman you settled down for, that you built a life with. Another reason why Adem had been perfect for her. Despite his own fears and apprehensions, he'd put aside every reason not to and jumped at the chance to have Sadie with him for life.

Even if that had turned out to be far shorter than any of them had imagined.

No, Dylan wasn't the man to replace Adem in her life, if anyone even could. He couldn't commit to forever, and he knew that Sadie deserved nothing less. And even if he wanted to try...what would it do to her, not to mention Finn, when he failed? It wasn't worth the risk.

But he could offer her something else. After all the sorrow and stress in her life over the last couple of years, he could see shoots of new growth in her—the first hints of spring ready to return to Sadie's world. She was ready to get out there again, to blossom into a new life.

He could be a friend and business partner in that new life. But right now, in this brief time of transition, maybe he could be something more. Something temporary. A first step, perhaps. Something that would waken that new Sadie completely.

It might be the worst idea he'd ever had—and if he told Neal what he had planned he had no doubt his old friend would be on the first plane out there to stop him. But it had been over a decade now—thirteen years of watching her, wanting her and wondering about her. Who could really blame him for wanting to taste that forbidden fruit, just once, now he knew how much she wanted it too?

Just one night. How bad a sin would that be, really? As long as he was honest and upfront with her, and they both knew what they were getting out of it. They were adults now. If Sadie knew exactly what he was offering, she could make her own decision.

It just might take a while for her to talk herself into it, knowing Sadie.

He watched her lean legs disappearing into the water and shifted to keep a better eye on her as she dived under the waves. She looked so at home out there, like a sea nymph returning to her natural environment after being cooped up on land for too long. She looked free in a way she hadn't since he'd arrived in Turkey.

Dylan wanted to make her look that way on land. Preferably in a bed.

Eventually, Sadie emerged again from the waves, slicking her dark hair back from her face with her hands. With water droplets shining off her skin in the sun, she began walking back towards him, and Dylan found himself putting a lot of effort into keeping his body calm and relaxed in the face of such a sight. God, she was beautiful.

The sound of his ringing phone was an almost welcome distraction. Fumbling in the pocket of his rucksack, he pulled it out and answered, only half listening to what his assistant had to say as Sadie arrived, rolled her eyes at him, and began towelling off with a spare towel.

By the time he ended the call Dylan wasn't entirely sure what he'd agreed to, but he trusted his assistant to email him all the pertinent details. He'd deal with them later, when there were fewer distractions around.

'Honestly. Who brings work to the beach?' Wrapping a flimsy scarf thing around her waist, Sadie dropped to sit on the towel beside him.

'You brought me,' Dylan pointed out. 'This week, that's practically the same thing.'

Sadie laughed, high and bright, a sound he'd almost thought lost. She was so much more relaxed out here; he could tell it from the lines of her shoulders, the absence of the crease between her eyebrows that he'd thought was permanent. This was the Sadie he remembered.

'Seriously, though,' she said, 'what's so important that it can't wait a few hours? Why not just let it ring—or, better yet, turn it off?'

Dylan shrugged—and realised she was watching his shoulders rise and fall. Interesting. 'Guess I don't want to risk missing an opportunity. I've missed too many in my life already.'

He'd been talking about the years spent taking responsibility for his family, saying no to chances and opportunities because they'd needed him. But as the words hung in the air between them he realised she thought he meant something else entirely. And maybe, he admitted to himself, maybe he did. *Did you ever wonder what might have happened if you'd met me first, instead of Adem?*

I wondered.

Sadie looked down at her hands, damp hair hanging forward across her cheek. 'I'm not the same girl you asked that question all those years ago,' she said, her voice soft.

'You think I don't know that?' he asked. 'Look at me, Sadie.' She did as he asked, and Dylan took a long moment just absorbing everything she was now. Slowly, obviously, he looked over every inch of her, from her hair—shorter now than when they'd met by a good foot—down over her body, past every added curve or line, every soft patch and every muscle, all the way to her feet.

Did she really not know? Not realise how much she'd grown up since then—and how every year had only made her a better person? Who would want the twenty-year-old Sadie compared to the one who sat before him now?

'You are so much more now than you were then,' he murmured, knowing she'd hear him anyway. 'You're stronger, more beautiful, more alive...more than I ever dreamt any woman could be.'

Sadie stared down at him, captivated by his gaze as confusion, guilt and hope fought for space in her head. Did he really think that?

Yes. The answer came fast and true as she looked into his eyes. This wasn't Dylan making a move, the way he did with all those other women. This wasn't a seduction attempt. It was him stating a fact—something that was true and obvious to him, even if she found it hard to believe.

The knowledge that he believed it warmed her damp skin far more than the sun overhead. And his gaze on her body...well, that felt even hotter.

She broke, forcing her gaze away from his, and reached for a dry towel to lay out on the sand. Whatever this was between them, she wasn't ready to deal with it

just yet. She needed time to process his words—to ex-
amine them, pick them apart and find some sense in
them, somewhere. And that was all but impossible when
he was lying there next to her in nothing but a pair of
swim shorts.

'You should go for a swim,' she said, not looking at
him. 'The water's glorious.'

'You looked very happy, splashing about out there.'
He didn't make any move towards the water, though.

'I love it,' Sadie admitted. A truth for a truth perhaps.
'The sea always makes me feel…free somehow.' Like
all her promises and commitments, all her obligations
and the weight of her worries might just float away on
the tide.

'I can see the appeal.' With a groan, Dylan hauled
himself to his feet, brushing off the stray grains of sand
that clung to his legs. 'Okay. I'll go for a swim.' He
flashed her a smile. 'Just for you.'

'Great. Enjoy.' Sadie sat down on her fresh towel with
a bump, staring after him as he walked towards the water's edge, the sun turning his skin golden across his
broad back and trim waist.

She needed to think, she reminded herself, not ogle.
With an act of willpower much harder than it should have
been, she lay down and closed her eyes. There was no
way she could think sensibly about that strange moment
with Dylan while she could still see him. His very presence was distracting.

Unfortunately, she'd failed to account for her late night
and exercise in her plan. The next thing she knew, cool
droplets of water were dripping onto her and a sun-warm
towel was being laid across her body. Her eyes flew open
to find out why.

'Sorry.' Dylan tossed his head back, sending more

water droplets flying. 'But it's pretty warm out here. I was afraid you'd burn.'

Personally, Sadie thought his presence might be more of a threat of that than the sun, but she wasn't telling him that.

'Thanks.' She sat up. 'Good swim? How long was I asleep?'

Dylan shrugged, fished in his bag for his phone and checked the time. 'Half an hour or so, I guess? It's nearly two.'

'Wow. We missed lunch. Are you hungry?' It wasn't like they hadn't had a substantial breakfast to keep them going, but all of a sudden her stomach was grumbling.

'You know, amazingly, I am.'

'Come on, then. There's a great seafood place just off the beach. And it's in the shade.'

Together, they packed up their small camp. Sadie pulled on her skirt and top over her tankini, and breathed a sigh of relief as Dylan put his shirt back on too. Half-naked Dylan on the beach was one thing—sitting at lunch was another entirely.

They headed up towards the boardwalk that ran along the edge of the beach. Brushing dry sand from their feet, they put their shoes back on and Sadie led him past the first few restaurants and cafés to the one she had in mind.

'Finn loves the seafood platters here,' she said, as they waited to be shown to a table. 'You'd think a four-year-old would balk at calamari and battered prawns and such, but he loves them.'

'It's sounding pretty good to me too,' Dylan said. 'Perfect for a light lunch after a morning on the beach.'

Sadie smiled up at him. 'Then that's what we'll have.'

Their table was at the front of the restaurant, and the glass doors that spanned the length of the space had been thrown open. Sadie sat back and listened to the waves, enjoying the cool shade on her hot body as they waited for their food. Her skin felt almost too sensitive now, like it was still being touched all over. She glanced across the table at Dylan and found his eyes already on her.

Maybe that was why.

It wasn't until they were tucking into their seafood platter that Sadie spotted the small flaw in her plan. 'I was going to take you out for seafood tonight,' she said, remembering suddenly her booking at the restaurant on the marina that had such good reviews. It was fancier than this place, and probably had less sand on the floor, but she'd be willing to bet their seafood platter wouldn't have been as good as the one they were enjoying anyway. 'Guess I'd better come up with something else after this. What do you fancy?'

Dylan paused with a prawn halfway to his mouth, looking at her just a moment too long to be entirely comfortable.

'Actually, I've got plans for tonight.'

Oh. How stupid to assume that he'd want to spend the whole day with her and have dinner too. Just because he had the previous day.

'Plans for us,' Dylan clarified, and relief warred with anxiety within her.

'Oh?' she said, as lightly as she could. 'I thought *I* was supposed to be showing *you* the town.'

'And you've been doing a great job,' he said. 'But now it's my turn.'

'Where are we going?' Sadie asked, because she couldn't really ask 'Is this a date?' without sounding incredibly idiotic if it wasn't—and terrified if it was.

'It's a surprise.' Dylan's smile was almost wolfish, and it sent a shiver across the surface of her skin. 'Just dress fancy, be in the lobby at eight, and leave everything else to me.'

Leave everything to him? If Dylan was in charge she shouldn't be worried about it being a date.

She should be scared—or prepared—for it to be a seduction.

CHAPTER NINE

BACK AT THE AZURE, Dylan hung behind as they arrived in the lobby, waiting for Sadie to disappear before he put his last-minute plan into action.

It only took a moment to realise that Sadie was doing exactly the same thing. The woman was incurably curious.

'Go on,' he said, making a shooing motion with his hands. 'You go get yourself all dolled up for tonight.'

'You're sure?' Sadie remained hovering next to the reception desk, her hands clasped in front of her. Behind the desk, the woman on Reception rolled her eyes in amusement. 'You don't need me to call and book anything? What about a taxi?'

'I have it all in hand,' Dylan assured her. Which was only partially a lie—he knew exactly what he needed to do to get it in hand. Sadie just had to leave the area first. 'And if I don't, the lovely...' He waved at the girl behind the desk.

'Esma,' she filled in promptly.

'Esma here can help me. So go. Get ready.' For a moment he thought she was about to object again, then she nodded sharply and started to head for the lifts.

He should let her go. Anything else would just make her more curious, more determined to find out his plans. But still...

'And, Sadie?' he called after her. She paused and turned back to face him. 'Don't wear black tonight.'

Sadie's frustrated expression was its own reward.

Once he was sure she'd really gone, and the lift lights had ticked up to the higher floors, Dylan turned to Esma.

'Okay, here's the thing. I have a plan, but I need a little help.'

'Whatever you need, sir,' Esma replied cheerfully, and he wondered if she'd been ordered to give him anything he wanted, just to make sure he invested. Probably, he decided. No one who worked with people all day was ever naturally that cheery by late afternoon.

'Great,' he said. 'Here's what I need...'

A few phone calls later and it was done. Cars booked—thanks to Sadie's reminder about taxis—and the best table reserved at the restaurant of the swankiest and newest hotel in Kuşadasi. As an afterthought, he'd also booked a room. Not—despite the voice at the back of his head telling him what a great idea it would be—to try and convince Sadie that friendship wasn't enough.

No, if Sadie was serious about coming up with a new plan, and doing whatever it took to save the Azure, then she needed to know what she was up against. And so did he. The Paradise Grand Hotel was the place to go for that. By the time she'd taken a good look at the place and its rooms and restaurant, Sadie would know exactly how much work they had ahead of them.

Letting himself into his suite, he headed straight for the shower, whistling as he went. Everything was coming together nicely.

It wasn't until he was lathering up, water sluicing down around him, that it occurred to Dylan that *Sadie* might think the evening could be something other than just business.

And would that really be so bad?

They'd made it past the memories of last night and through the strange, close moments on the beach. If he wasn't mistaken, there had been a definite…softening in Sadie's attitude to him since he'd confessed to the almost-kiss she apparently couldn't remember.

Maybe this *was* more than just business. Maybe it could even be a second chance at something he'd never really had a first chance at.

But no. Tonight wasn't the night.

Even if he did want to try and win one night with her, one glorious stolen moment, it couldn't be tonight. Before anything at all could happen between them, they had to hammer out the work side of things. Mixing business and pleasure never ended well, in his experience.

But once their plan for the Azure was secure, he'd have a whole new proposal to put to Sadie.

He couldn't just take his usual, casual approach to a hook-up—because Sadie wasn't like his usual conquests. They had history, for a start. And she'd been clear on the friendship front, for good reasons. Her place was here in Turkey, with Finn and her memories, much as he wished he might be able to persuade her to move on from that. He couldn't compete with the commitments she'd made—and even if he could, would he really want to? So he'd be upfront about what he could offer—and it wasn't forever. He was a short-term fix at best—in business or otherwise. That had to be clear before he could take things further, otherwise it wouldn't be fair—on either of them.

Tonight would be all business.

Decision made, Dylan shut off the shower and told himself that putting on his best suit for the evening was all about the destination, not the company.

* * *

Don't wear black. What kind of fashion advice was that? And who was Dylan Jacobs to tell her what she should or shouldn't wear anyway?

Except…if tonight was about them for once, instead of business, maybe this was just his way of hinting at that. Letting her know she was off duty tonight; that she could retire the black suit, relax and just enjoy being there with him.

She had to admit it did sound appealing.

Eventually, she picked out a navy halterneck cocktail dress that showed off her slightly pink shoulders, and slid it over her showered and lotioned skin. It was fancier than anything she'd have worn to the restaurant at the Azure or to a bar, but not too over the top. And he had said to dress up…

With a decisive nod, Sadie picked out her highest silver heels and added a little eyeliner to her usual make-up.

When she finally made her way down to the lobby, she was glad she'd made the effort. Hanging off the arm of Dylan Jacobs could be enough to make a girl feel positively plain by comparison at the best of times, but the suit he'd chosen for the evening only made things worse. Charcoal grey and perfectly cut, it accentuated all the wonderful things about his body that she'd tried not to stare at on the beach that morning. With a crisp, white shirt open at the neck he looked the epitome of relaxed elegance.

Sadie stood up a little straighter and hoped she didn't fall over in the unfamiliar heels.

'You look fantastic,' Dylan said, leaning in to kiss her cheek. 'And navy—'

'It's not black,' Sadie interrupted quickly. 'That was your only stipulation.'

'Is definitely your colour—that was all I was going to say.' Dylan flashed her a smile as he took her arm. 'Come on, the car is waiting.'

'Okay,' Sadie said, once they were both settled in the back seat of the car. 'I'm dolled up, we're in the car—*now* will you tell me where we're going?'

'What's the best, most luxurious and prestigious hotel in Kuşadasi?'

'The new Paradise Grand,' Sadie answered promptly, then frowned. 'Wait. Why are we going there?'

'To check out the competition,' Dylan said. 'If you're really ready to go with a new plan to save the Azure, you need to know exactly what you're up against.'

She should have worn a black suit.

Hopefully the car was dark enough that he couldn't see her embarrassed blush. What had she been thinking, imagining this could be anything more than just business? Wasn't that what they'd agreed? And what she'd insisted on from the start?

This was why he was here, in Turkey. Anything else was completely incidental. She had to remember that.

'Here we are,' Dylan said a while later, as the car pulled to a halt. Jumping out, he headed round to open her door before the driver could, and she took his hand as she stepped out of the car.

At least now she knew what she was really there for, she could give it her full attention.

The new Paradise Grand Hotel was on the outskirts of town, a little further than most tourists would like—but there the similarities with the Azure ended. Sadie was pretty sure that any guest would put up with the mildly inconvenient location in return for the splendour the Paradise Grand offered.

The hotel building rose out of a garden of palm leaves

and greenery, all glass and steel and white stone. Her hand on Dylan's arm, Sadie climbed the steps and the automatic doors opened with a swoosh.

Inside, the lobby was every bit as impressive as the exterior. The centre of the building was open all the way to the glass roof—some twenty storeys up—and every floor had a balcony overlooking the majesty of the central foyer. An ostentatious fountain burbled in the middle, surrounded by more local flora. Sadie swallowed as the chattering sounds of what had to be a full-occupancy hotel filled her ears.

Yeah, nothing like the Azure at all.

They were led through to the elevators by one of the several concierges, then up to the restaurant on the top floor. Their table, Sadie was hardly even surprised to note at this point, was right by the window, looking out over the town of Kuşadasi and the ocean beyond.

She wondered if she could see the Azure from there…

'So, what do you think?' Dylan asked, after the waiter had taken their wine order and left them to peruse the menu.

Sadie shook her head. 'The Azure is nothing like this.' And, quite honestly, she wouldn't want it to be. Yes, the Paradise Grand was impressive, and luxurious—but it wasn't her dream. Or Adem's.

'That's because this place is brand-new,' Dylan said. 'Shiny as the day it came out of the box. That's what some customers want.'

'But not all.'

'No, not all.' He leant back in his seat, looking out over the admittedly glorious view. 'But before you decide what your customers want, you need to know what *you* want. If it isn't this, fine. But what is it? What do you want the Azure to be? What makes it special to you? What's the big dream?'

Wasn't that the million Turkish lire question? The one she knew she *should* know the answer to already.

But she didn't. Because it had always been Adem's dream, not hers. She'd gone along with it, listened, been supportive, helped where she could…but she couldn't say what the goal was or the vision, because he'd held all that in his head. All she had were the plans he'd left behind and they'd already established that they weren't enough.

'Adem wanted…' she started, but Dylan shook his head.

'I'm not interested in what Adem wanted for the place. If you truly want to save it, to give it a new future against competition like this, it has to be *your* dream. Not his.'

Sadie stared at him, knowing he was right but still not knowing the answers.

How could she admit to him that her commitment to the Azure had more to do with memories of the past than the future?

Watching her, sitting across the table in that beautiful dress, her shoulders bare and her skin golden in the candlelight, Dylan wished heartily that this could be what it must look like to outsiders—a romantic meal for two. But he was in Turkey to do a job—to help her. And he couldn't let his personal wants get in the way of her very urgent business needs.

Not yet, anyway.

Still, seeing her struggle to answer what should have been the first question he'd asked on arrival, he wished more than anything that wasn't the case.

'I…I don't know,' Sadie finally admitted, the frustration in her expression showing him exactly how much those words had cost her.

'Okay. Try this,' he said. 'Imagine yourself at the Azure in five years' time. How does it look? What's its best features?'

'Five years...' Sadie's eyelids fluttered closed as she considered. 'Finn would be ten.'

Finn. He'd asked her to think about the business, and she'd instantly thought of her son. Dylan frowned. What was he missing here?

'Sadie,' he said, and her eyes flew open again. His gaze locked onto hers, and he knew this was his best chance to get at the truth. 'Tell me honestly. Why do you want to save the Azure?'

'For Finn,' she said, the words coming so quickly he knew she hadn't had to think about them at all. 'Because it's the only thing left of his father that I can give him. It's Adem's legacy.'

A noble reason, but Dylan knew it wouldn't be enough. She had to want it for herself, too. 'What about you?'

'I...I love the spa. That was always *my* place, *my* dream. But the hotel...it was all Adem.' He'd suspected as much, but from the relief that shone out of Sadie's face he had a feeling this was the first time she'd admitted to herself that, in truth, she didn't really want to be there. 'To be honest, without him there, some days it's hard to remember why I stay at all.'

'Sadie...' Dylan's heart clenched at the loss and confusion in her voice. No wonder the place was crumbling all around her. A project as big as the Azure needed love, not just obligation. It needed passion, not just vague enthusiasm. It needed what Adem had felt for it, and Sadie obviously didn't.

'I shouldn't have said that.' Sadie shook her head, as

if she could wipe away the words with the movement. The waiter arrived with their wine, and she took a large gulp the moment he'd tasted it and it had been poured.

'Are you ready to—?' the waiter started.

'Another few minutes, please.' Neither of them had so much as looked at the menu yet. Besides, he wasn't going to let Sadie use ordering food as an excuse to drop this line of conversation. Not when there was so much more to say.

As the waiter backed unobtrusively away, Dylan fixed Sadie with a determined look. 'You were saying?'

She took a deep breath before answering. He wondered if that was a sign that what was coming was a lie. He wasn't used to Sadie lying—or perhaps he'd just never noticed her lies before.

'The Azure is a wonderful hotel,' she said. 'It has huge potential, plenty of history and an awful lot going for it businesswise. But more than that, it's our future—mine and Finn's, I mean. It's my son's inheritance. And I'm committed to saving it.'

'Even though it's not your dream?' She didn't understand. Sometimes commitment wasn't enough. Sometimes commitment made people miserable, made them yell and scream and cry—until they just gave up on it and walked away, like his father had done.

He really didn't want to see that happen to Sadie.

'Only little girls believe that dreams will come true.' There was a scathing note in Sadie's voice, but Dylan ignored it. Because he knew different.

Sadie had believed in dreams once. He'd seen it in her eyes the day she'd shown him her engagement ring for the first time, and again on her wedding day. The first time she'd held out her baby son to meet him. She'd believed in happily ever after, in possibilities and greatness, even if she'd wanted them all with another man.

Finally, he'd found something about new Sadie he didn't like as much as old Sadie.

He sighed. How to make her understand? 'Look. I could give you all the money your current business plan calls for. I could help you come up with a new plan and fund that instead. I could bulldoze the Azure and rebuild it from the ground up, if you decided that was what you wanted. But none of it will make a bit of difference if you don't want it enough.'

'I just told you I—'

'Commitment and obligation aren't enough,' he interrupted her. 'You're not a multinational conglomerate, and you're not trying to build a heartless, soulless place like the Paradise Grand. The Azure is about charm, heart and home—those are its selling points. The personal touch. And if it's not home to you, if you don't love it...' He shook his head.

'So you're saying you won't help me.' Sadie straightened her cutlery beside her napkin and avoided his gaze.

'I'm not saying that,' he said. 'But I want you to really think about what it is you want, whether the Azure truly is your home, before we go any further with this.'

It was a risk—both personally and professionally. He was testing her commitments to the past and, knowing how she'd felt about Adem, it was entirely possible she was going to send him packing. So, yeah, big risk.

But he knew it was also the right thing to do. The only thing.

As the tension stretched between them he reached for his menu and opened it.

'Come on, let's order. That very discreet and professional waiter over there has been hovering for at least the last ten minutes.'

Sadie nodded, and turned to the first page of her own menu, but he wasn't sure she was actually reading it at all. Instead, she looked completely lost in thought.

Dylan just hoped that they were good thoughts.

Sadie ate her meal in silence and, for once, Dylan seemed content to let her. Maybe he knew she had too much to think about to make conversation at the same time. Or maybe he was just preoccupied with whatever message had flashed up on his phone. Either way, he didn't seem particularly interested in her.

So much for her thoughts that tonight might be more than just business. She really should have known better.

The worst part was admitting that, for a moment, she'd hoped it could be something more. That maybe, just maybe, this might be a chance for her to start moving on. To follow Rachel's advice and get back out there. A totally out of character, one-night stand to reboot her chances at romance. Just this once.

Dylan was the king of short-term flings. If she wanted something short and sweet to kick-start her new life, he'd be perfect. As long as they could be upfront about what it was and wasn't, and could keep it separate from business.

But it seemed that *nothing* trumped business for Dylan.

As she finished up her last mouthful of dessert— which was, she had to admit, delicious—Sadie pushed the plate aside and prepared to call time on an altogether depressing evening. Not only had she completely misread Dylan's intentions, the more time she spent at the Paradise Grand, the more convinced she became that the Azure could never be anything like this.

'Do you have a car booked back to the Azure,' she asked, 'or shall I get the concierge to call us a taxi while we pay for dinner? They can take a while on busy nights.'

Dylan looked up from his phone and grinned. 'Sorry, am I ignoring you?'

Sadie shook her head. 'I'm just thinking about getting back to work.'

'Actually, there's one more thing I want to see here first.' He slipped his phone back into his jacket pocket and smiled again, slower this time. Sexier. With his full attention on her, Sadie couldn't stop the warmth that seemed to cover her skin under his gaze. Really, who could blame a girl for getting ideas when he looked at her like that?

'What's that?' she asked, but Dylan was already standing.

'Let me settle up here,' he said, eyes dark with promise. 'Then you'll find out.' He flashed her one last smile as he signalled the waiter over, and Sadie swallowed despite her suddenly dry throat.

Get a grip, Sadie, she told herself firmly. She was imagining things. He'd made it perfectly clear that tonight was about business only. Nothing he did next would convince her otherwise.

Or so she thought, until he led her out of the restaurant to the elevator, stopping at the twelfth floor and pulling out a room key card.

'You got us a room?' she asked, as he slipped the key card into the lock and, with a flash of green, the door fell open. He stood aside to let her in, and Sadie entered, staring around her. 'A room with champagne. And rose petals. And chocolates.'

Okay, maybe she hadn't been entirely imagining the vibes. After all, who booked a hotel suite complete with built-in seduction supplies if they didn't have plans other than business for the night?

In a split second Sadie made her decision. Even the fear and anxiety burning through her veins couldn't compete with the rising tension between them. For twelve years she'd wondered what it would feel like to kiss Dylan Jacobs—and since the moment in the elevator after their night on the town that curiosity had grown beyond all reasonable proportions.

He wanted her. What more proof did she need than rose petals on the coverlet and champagne chilling beside the huge king-sized bed? Maybe he'd just wanted to get business out of the way before they moved on to the more...personal part of the evening. She could understand that, even if she wished he'd shared his plans with her earlier. Except she'd never have concentrated on work if she'd known she had this waiting for her.

And, God, why was she still thinking?

Sucking in a breath, she turned, only to find Dylan right behind her. Her hands came up automatically to rest against his chest and she looked up to see heat in his eyes. No doubt at all, he wanted this too.

'You booked us a room.' Her voice barely sounded like hers—it was too breathy, too sultry.

Dylan nodded, his gaze fixed on hers like she held all the power here for once. Sadie kind of liked it.

Seizing the moment, she stretched up onto her toes, bringing her mouth just millimetres away from his, savouring every moment. 'Good idea,' she murmured, and leaned in to kiss him.

From the moment their lips touched, bliss filled Sadie. Every inch of her body fizzed from finally, finally kissing Dylan Jacobs. And she knew, in her heart, that this was right—that she could move on, that there was a future for her beyond always being a widow. That she was still a woman, too.

Until Dylan stepped back, breaking the kiss, his hands on her upper arms holding her away.

'Sadie…no, I'm sorry…'

Normally, the sight of Dylan lost for words would have amused her. As it was, it just enraged her.

He'd ruined her fizz.

'If you tell me you booked this room to compare it to the Azure…'

'I didn't ask for the champagne and stuff!' He waved an arm around wildly, encompassing the room. 'They must have…misunderstood.'

'Just like me.' Sadie bit the words out, too furious to say more.

'No! I… It's just, this needs to be business first between us, Sadie.'

Because everything was, for him, wasn't it? Nothing mattered more than the next project, the next shining opportunity. Certainly not her.

'Of course.' With a deep breath, Sadie gathered the tattered remains of her dignity around her, and gave thanks that she hadn't wasted her best red dress on this disaster of an evening. 'Well, I think I've seen all I need to here. If you'll excuse me…'

She didn't care if he had a car booked or plans to look through some slideshow on the Azure's future. Sadie was going to the bar, drinking one more glass of wine to wipe away this evening, then getting a cab back home, where she would go straight to bed. No champagne, no rose petals, no Dylan. Alone.

'Sadie, wait.' He tried to grab her arm again, but she dodged him.

'I'll see you in the lobby in the morning as normal,'

she said. Maybe if she pretended nothing had happened tonight, he'd forget—like she had, apparently, after that wedding so many years ago. 'We've got plenty of work ahead of us.'

And that was all. Just work.

CHAPTER TEN

THIS NEEDS TO be business...

Sadie woke with the same words echoing in her head that she'd fallen asleep to, and a familiar burn of embarrassment coursing through her body.

What on earth had she been thinking, trying to kiss Dylan? Maybe she could just blame the wine.

Lying back against her pillows, she ran through the night before in her head. The part before everything had gone crazy and wrong. There had to be something she could salvage from her utter humiliation.

The business message had certainly got through loud and clear. So, how did she show him that she was back to work mode today, and that last night had been a minor blip? What had he told her she needed to do to live up to the luxuries of the Paradise Grand?

The other hotel had certainly been impressive, she had to admit, and the food *almost* as good as the Azure's. But it didn't feel homely or comfortable...

Suddenly, Dylan's words came back to her.

'The Azure is about charm, heart and home—those are its selling points. The personal touch. And if it's not home to you, if you don't love it...'

Maybe he had a point.

In fact, she decided as she headed for the shower, even

if last night hadn't been exactly what she'd been hoping for, maybe it had given her something more. Not another notch on Dylan's bedpost, which in the cold morning light she could only agree was a good thing. She'd lost her mind, briefly, but she was back in control now. This was all a business proposal—not a fantasy romance or a glimpse of possibilities that never really were.

Instead, he'd given her a way to prove to him, once and for all, that he should invest. All he wanted to know was that this place truly was her home, her passion.

And she knew exactly how to do that.

Suddenly, the day didn't seem quite so hopeless.

She met him in the lobby as usual, knowing he'd clocked her casual dress immediately. His eyebrows rose, just a touch, as he smiled a greeting at her. Was that nervousness she saw behind his eyes?

'So, boss lady, what's the plan for today?' Boss lady. He really wanted to make sure she didn't forget this was business, didn't he? Well, that was just fine by her.

'Have you eaten breakfast?' she asked, too focussed on her plan for small talk.

'Sort of.' His forehead crinkled up a little in confusion. 'Some fruit and cereal. I wasn't all that hungry after last night's feast. Why?'

'Perfect,' she said, ignoring the question. 'You don't want a heavy stomach for today's activities.'

'Now I'm really intrigued,' Dylan admitted.

Sadie flashed him a bright, fake smile. 'Good. Then follow me.'

He'd seen the whole hotel on their tour on the first day, so by the time she'd led him down the stone stairs and towards the corridor to the spa he'd already figured it out, which shouldn't really have surprised her. He was a bright guy.

'A spa day?' he asked, a hint of incredulity in his voice.

'The spa is one of the Azure's biggest attractions,' she reminded him, as they reached the heavy wooden door that led to her own personal sanctuary. 'It makes sense for you to spend some time here, see what all the fuss is about.' She pushed the door open, the heady scent of oils and steam filling her lungs as she stepped through. 'Besides, you'll need to lock your phone up in the lockers here. It'll do you good to switch off from your other business and concentrate on the Azure for a few hours.'

'I need to stay in touch with the office—' Dylan started, but she cut him off, more determined than ever.

'Not today. You want proof that the Azure is a safe investment? I'm about to give it to you. So I want you paying attention.'

'If you insist.' Dylan sighed, and followed her through the door to the spa reception desk. 'Okay, I'm game. So, what? You're going to give me a massage?'

Sadie wished she could blame the heat in her cheeks on the higher temperature of the spa rooms. Sadly, she knew herself better than that.

'Not me. We have an excellent trained staff here to see to your every need. But I'll show you around first, explain the different rooms to you.' Smiling at the spa receptionist, Andreas, she added, 'Andreas here will take you through to the male changing rooms and lockers, show you where everything is. I'll meet you on the other side.'

Slipping through to the women's changing rooms, Sadie didn't waste time, stripping off to her swimming costume quickly and locking everything up in her personal locker. Wrapping a robe around herself, she headed straight through to the spa, pleased to beat Dylan there by even a few moments. He looked faintly uncomfortable in the fluffy white robe, the towelling material making his shoulders look broader than ever. Still, she decided, it was good for him to go outside his comfort zone now and then.

He looked around him and Sadie watched his face for reactions as he took in the creamy marble, with hints of brown and rust red, which covered the walls. Above them, a domed and mural-painted roof belied their location underneath the hotel, making them appear to be in some ancient Turkish bath instead. The soothing splash of water from the pools toned nicely with the gentle music playing over the hidden speakers.

'So, where do we start?' Dylan asked.

'With the Turkish bath, of course,' Sadie said.

If that didn't relax him into handing over the cash, nothing would.

'This is the warm room,' Sadie explained, as she paused by a steamed-up glass door and slipped off her robe, hanging it up. 'Traditionally, this is where you would start a proper Turkish bath.'

She pushed the door open and Dylan shucked his own robe and followed her through, silently cursing the steam that rose up and obscured the beautiful curve of her behind in her swimsuit.

It had taken every grain of restraint in his body not to kiss her back the night before—and now she was tormenting him with *this*. A whole day in her barely clad company, trying to *relax*. And she'd made it perfectly clear it was all business. Just the way he'd wanted it.

The woman was a demon.

Inside, the warm room was empty of other people—which Dylan appreciated. Sadie took a seat on the tiled bench seat that ran around the outer edge of the room, and he followed suit, choosing to sit opposite her instead of beside her—something he regretted when he realised the steam hid her almost completely now.

He shuffled round a little closer, until he could make out the outline of her face at least.

'So, what do we do here?' he asked, settling back as the heat rolled over him, the steam already dripping off his skin as well as the wall behind him.

'We sit. We relax.' Sadie sounded different here already, like her words could take their time coming out. Like there was no rush for anything any more.

Dylan fidgeted, switching position to try to get a little more comfortable against the tile. 'That's it?'

'That's it,' Sadie said, apparently very satisfied with that state of affairs.

She'd tilted her head back against the wall, and as far as he could tell her eyes were closed. He watched the beads of water roll down the long line of her neck for a moment. No sign that she found this in any way frustrating. Clearly, she was enjoying the peace and quiet.

He gave it a minute before he decided that was too bad. He had questions.

'So, is this a traditional Turkish spa?'

'Yes and no,' Sadie answered, without moving or opening her eyes. 'I wanted to incorporate some of the aspects of a traditional Turkish bath, but I knew I couldn't compete with the authentic Turkish baths in the town. So, instead, I decided to go with a spa that would feel familiar to the visiting tourists—especially the Western ones—but would still feel a little exotic, too.'

'The best of both worlds.'

'That's the idea.'

Listening to her talk, even absently, about the plans she'd had for this place, it was easy to see exactly what was missing in her plans for the Azure. Here, she'd known instinctively what she wanted to do, what was important to the guests, what would work well. This was her comfort zone. The hotel wasn't.

Tilting his head back to copy Sadie, he stared up at the mosaic-domed roof, picking out patterns through the steam. Then, when that grew boring, he went back to watching Sadie instead.

She looked so much more relaxed here. Like she had swimming in the sea the day before. She truly was a water nymph.

'When was the last time you came down here?' he asked. 'Not just in a suit to check on the business either.'

'Too long,' Sadie admitted, turning her head to smile at him. 'I think everyone needs a day in the spa now and then.'

Her eyes fluttered shut again, and he followed suit, trying to find the same boneless relaxation she seemed to here. Letting the heat seep into his bones and the steam soak his skin, he let his shoulders drop and his mind zone out.

Maybe there was something to this relaxation malarkey after all.

Almost too soon, Sadie stirred beside him. 'Okay, time for the hot room.' She stood, gracefully.

Dylan peeled himself away from the tile with rather less finesse. 'This wasn't hot?'

'This was nothing,' Sadie told him, opening the door.

The hot room felt even hotter after the brief blast of normal spa temperature between the two rooms, but they didn't stay in the second room as long, which he appreciated. As they emerged back into the main spa, Sadie plunged herself into the circular pool in the centre of the room, letting the water sluice over her.

With a shrug, Dylan followed suit.

The ice-cold water hit his overheated skin like a thousand pins, and he rose gasping out of the water to find Sadie already out and perched on a wooden recliner beside it. She, somehow, managed to look refreshed and a little smug. Clearly this was revenge for the night before.

'You could have warned me.' He levered himself back out of the pool and reached for the towel she held out to him,

'Where would be the fun in that?' The impish gleam in her eyes made it hard to even pretend to be mad at her.

'Where indeed?' He sat down on the recliner next to her. 'Well, this has been lovely, but—'

'Oh, we're not done yet,' Sadie interrupted him.

'We're not?' Dylan shook his head, cold water droplets falling from his hair. 'What's next?'

'Traditionally, you'd be scrubbed clean by a bath assistant,' Sadie said. 'But today I think we'll let you off with just the massage. You can meet me in the pool afterwards.'

As a member of the spa staff, neatly dressed in white shorts and polo shirt, appeared to lead him to the massage room, Dylan saw another approach Sadie with a clipboard in hand. In a moment, all the relaxation he'd seen in her disappeared as she frowned at the paper in front of her, shoulders stiff.

'This way, sir,' the staff member said again, and Dylan hurried to catch up.

Left alone to settle face down onto the massage table, with just a small towel covering what was left of his modesty, Dylan tuned out the tasteful music and thought instead about Sadie.

She seemed so in control there in the spa—utterly unlike the uncertainty he saw in her when she talked about the hotel itself. Obviously, that was why she'd brought him there—to demonstrate that there was one place she felt totally at home here in Turkey. Here, she had passion and certainty.

The only problem with that was it just made it all the clearer that she didn't want to be running a hotel. She should be taking charge of a chain of spas, perhaps even in other hotels.

Maybe even in his new and burgeoning hotel chain.

Already the idea was taking hold, making him want to jump at the chance to make it happen. Sadie would have a career she truly dreamed of, and they could work together, seeing each other as often as possible...

But she'd have to leave the Azure. Break her commitment to Adem's dream. And there was the sticking point.

The door opened behind him, and Dylan stirred from his plotting as a familiar scent approached. He listened hard, recognising the pattern of her breath, the touch of her footfall.

Sadie.

Whatever she'd said about not giving him his massage, he had absolutely no doubt about who was standing behind him right now.

'Are you ready, sir?' she whispered, obviously trying to disguise her voice. 'I'm going to start with a simple massage. Let me know if the pressure is okay.'

She didn't want him to know it was her. But how could he not, when the first touch of her oiled fingers against his back made his whole body spark with excitement? Every movement she made was utterly professional—he'd never expect anything less from Sadie. But the feelings it left him with...

He was pretty sure that no massage in history had ever been less relaxing than this one.

* * *

This was torture. Actual cruel and unusual punishment for a crime she didn't fully remember committing.

Keeping her hands as smooth and steady as she could as they moved across the planes of Dylan's back, Sadie kept a running stream of mental curses going in her head. Mostly cursing the poor staff member who'd been sent home sick, leaving them short-handed. But partly cursing herself, too, for saying she'd take care of Dylan's massage.

She was the boss. She could have ordered anyone else to swap with her or take care of it. Instead, she'd decided to put herself through *this*.

She really was a glutton for punishment.

Staying professional, that was the key. It wasn't like she hadn't massaged beautiful people before, even a few famous ones. The trick was to treat them exactly the same way you'd treat anyone else. A body was just a body, when all was said and done, and they all needed the same care, love and attention to work away their worries and their aches.

It was just that *this* body was one she'd been thinking about for far longer than she cared to admit.

Focussing on the muscle groups helped, remembering every lesson she'd ever been taught about effective massage. She knew just where to press and where to hold back. She was *good* at this. She was a professional.

She was absolutely not thinking about what was underneath that very small towel.

Eventually, her time was up, and hopefully Dylan would never ask why he'd only had a back massage instead of a full-body one.

Stepping away, her heart still pumping too fast, Sadie murmured, 'I'll leave you to dress.'

'Thanks, Sadie.' His words were almost slurred, like he was too relaxed to articulate properly, but still they caused every muscle in her body to stiffen.

'How did you know?' she asked.

'I always know when you're near me.' Adjusting his towel to cover him, Dylan levered himself up and swung round to sit on the edge of the table. 'I always have.'

It was too much. The softness in his voice against the heat in his eyes. The implications of his words and the knowledge that just moments before she'd had her hands all over his body. Knowing that they were so close now he could touch her almost without moving. Her blood seemed too much and too hot for her body—hotter than it had ever been in any of the steam rooms.

All too, too much.

Business. That's all this was.

Sadie stepped back, away, and cleared her throat. 'Um, we have someone off sick, so I've been called in to cover. So I'll let you get on with enjoying the pool and so on. It'll be good for you to, uh, keep relaxing.'

Dylan nodded, slowly. 'Or maybe I'll just try the cold plunge pool again.'

'Whatever works.' She refused to think about why he might need the ice water, even for a moment.

'Will I see you for dinner?' he asked.

She wanted to say yes, but she couldn't. The wanting in his eyes…she knew exactly where that could lead, if they let it. And even if she'd thought last night that was what she wanted, seeing it now terrified her. This wasn't what she'd brought him to her spa for, not at all.

Dylan didn't do commitment, and she'd already committed too much. Wasn't that why she'd brought him there in the first place? To show him exactly how much she belonged at the Azure? So what good could come from giving in to those feelings now?

'Not tonight, I'm afraid,' she said, trying to sound apologetic. 'I need to type up my proposal for you, remember? But there's a Turkish night in the restaurant. I've booked you a table.'

'Fantastic.' Sadie ignored the total lack of enthusiasm in his voice. 'What about tomorrow?'

Tomorrow. His next-to-last day. She couldn't leave him alone again, but whatever they did needed to involve a lot more clothes than the last couple of days had. And preferably no easy access to a bed.

'Ephesus.' The word blurted out of her. 'I thought I'd take you to see the ruins at Ephesus.'

'Another big tourist attraction, I suppose.' How was his tone still so even, so steady when her own voice seemed to be getting squeakier by the second?

'The biggest. So, I'll see you in the lobby in the morning. Usual time.'

'If that's what you want.'

It wasn't. What she really wanted was to jump him, right here in the massage room. But what she needed to do was get back to work and put this whole afternoon behind her.

'It is.'

She'd do a shift in the spa, remind herself why she loved it so much. Then she'd spend the evening on Skype with Finn and her parents and dealing with the hotel admin.

She needed to remember all the things that *really* mattered in her world. And forget the feeling of Dylan's cool skin under her hands.

Or else she might go insane.

CHAPTER ELEVEN

DYLAN PACED THE lobby the next morning, waiting for Sadie. Who was late. Very late. For the first time since he'd arrived in Turkey.

Turning as he reached the automatic doors, too late to stop them opening for him, he headed back towards the large windows showcasing that brilliant view of the Aegean Sea. He tried to appreciate the view, but his mind was too preoccupied with wondering how the day was going to play out.

The rules had changed yesterday, that much had been obvious the moment he'd sat up on that massage table and looked into her eyes. The heat and want he'd seen reflected there had echoed his own so perfectly he couldn't help but think it was only a matter of time before they had to do something about it or explode. This wasn't a drunken attempt at a kiss in a lift, or a moment of madness brought on by a romantic hotel room. Sadie Sullivan wanted him, maybe as much as he wanted her. And despite every complication, every reason he knew he shouldn't, Dylan wasn't sure he'd make it out of Kuşadasi without doing something about that.

Except she was late, and he didn't know which Sadie was going to turn up today—buttoned-up business Sadie, old friend Sadie, or the Sadie who'd tried to kiss him the other night.

Yes, the rules had changed, to the point that Dylan wasn't even sure what game they were playing any more. If they were playing at all.

Ephesus. That was the plan for today. Ancient ruins, stones and sand and history. A big tourist draw, sure, but he couldn't shake the feeling that wasn't why Sadie was taking him there. More likely she was trying to get him somewhere safe—away from temptation and lost in someone else's history instead of their own.

Pity it would never work.

Besides, he wasn't interested in history today. He wanted to talk to her about the future.

Dylan had spent his solitary evening making plans, researching and brainstorming. He'd been looking for a way to set the hotel chain he'd recently taken over apart from the norm, and a spa range of the calibre of Sadie's could be just what he needed. Sure, it wasn't unique, but it *was* good and profitable, according to his preliminary research. He'd know more when his assistant got back to him with the stats and figures he'd requested.

Then he'd just need to talk to Sadie about it. He liked to hope she'd be excited about the new opportunity, but knowing Sadie he suspected that pulling her away from the old one would be the real challenge.

Turning to head back towards the doors, he caught sight of the Azure logo on the reception desk, and almost smiled. Just a few days ago seeing the name would have been enough to make him scowl. But now… Sadie had changed the way he thought about the Azure. About many things.

The lift dinged and the doors opened, revealing Sadie in a light and breezy sundress, a straw hat perched on her head. 'Sorry I'm late,' she said, without much apology in her voice. 'Let's get going.'

Dylan followed, trying not to read too much into the fact she'd barely looked at him.

In the car, Sadie switched the radio on before she even fastened her seat belt, turning the volume up high enough to make conversation next to impossible. Dylan smiled to himself as he settled into the passenger seat. So, that was the way she wanted to play it. Fine.

He was willing to bet there were no radios at Ephesus. She'd have to talk to him then—for a whole day, trapped inside some ancient ruins.

Of course, she'd probably try to just lecture him on the history of the place. Which was fine by Dylan; he knew she couldn't keep it up forever.

Eventually, they were going to have to talk about the heat between them.

Satisfied, he sat back to enjoy the drive, watching the foreign landscape skimming past the window. He had to admit Turkey was a gorgeous country.

Beside him, Sadie let out a little gasp—just a slight gulp of air, but enough to alarm him. All thoughts of the scenery forgotten, he jerked round to see what the matter was.

On the wheel, Sadie's knuckles were white, her fingers clinging so tight there was no blood left in them. Her face had turned entirely grey. But it was her eyes, wide and unfocussed, that worried him most.

'Sadie? What is it?' No response. The car kept rolling forward in its lane, falling behind the car in front as her foot slackened on the accelerator. 'You need to pull over. Sadie. Sadie!'

The sharpness in his voice finally got through to her

and, blinking, she flipped on the indicator. Dylan placed his hands over hers as she swerved onto the side of the road, ignoring the beeping horns of the cars behind them.

The car stalled to a stop, and Dylan let out a long breath as his heart rate started to stabilise. 'Okay. What just—?'

Before he could finish his sentence the driver's door flew open and Sadie flung herself out of the car, inches away from the passing traffic. Without thinking, Dylan followed suit, jumping out and rushing round to find her already leaning against the rear of the car.

He slowed, approaching her cautiously, like an unpredictable and possibly dangerous wild animal. God only knew what was going on with her, but he knew instinctively that this wasn't part of the game they'd been playing since he'd arrived. This was something else entirely.

She didn't stir as he got closer, so he risked taking her arm, leading her gently to the side of the car furthest from the road.

'Sit down,' he murmured, as softly as he could. 'Come on, Sadie. Sit down here and tell me what the matter is.'

Bonelessly, she slid down to the dry grass, leaning back against the metal of the car. Dylan crouched in front of her, his gaze never leaving her colourless face.

'What is it?' he asked again. 'What just happened?'

'I forgot…' Sadie's said, her voice faint and somehow very far away. 'How could I forget?'

'Forgot what, sweetheart?'

'That we'd have to drive this way. Past this place.'

'This place? Where are we?' Dylan glanced around him but, as far as he could tell, it was just some road. Any road.

Oh. He was an idiot.

'This is where it happened?' he asked.

Sadie nodded, the movement jerky. 'Adem was driving out to some meeting somewhere, I think. A truck lost control along this stretch…'

And his best friend had been squashed under it in his car. He hadn't stood a chance.

'I haven't been this way since it happened,' Sadie said, her gaze still focussed somewhere in the distance. 'When I suggested Ephesus…I wasn't thinking about this. I wasn't thinking about Adem.'

The guilt and pain in her voice made him wince—and feel all the worse because he had a pretty good idea exactly what she *had* been thinking about at that moment.

'We don't have to go on,' he said. 'We can just go back to the hotel. I can drive.'

But Sadie shook her head. 'No. I want… This is the worst of it. I just need to sit here for a moment. Is that…? Will you sit with me?'

'Of course.' He shuffled over to sit beside her and lifted his arm to wrap it around her as she rested her head against his shoulder. He couldn't offer her much right now, but any comfort he could give was hers. Always had been.

'It's crazy, really,' she said, the words slightly muffled by his shirt. 'That one place—one insignificant patch of road—can hold such power over me. There are no ruins here, no markers, no information boards. Just me, knowing that this…this is where he died.'

'We don't have to talk about it.'

'Maybe I do.' Sadie looked up, just enough to catch his gaze, and Dylan almost lost himself in the desolate depths of her eyes. 'I haven't, really. Haven't talked it out, or whatever it is you're supposed to do with the sort of grief that fills you up from the inside out until there's nothing left. I just…got on with things, I suppose.'

He could see it, all too easily. Could picture Sadie just throwing herself into the Azure, into making sure Finn was okay, and never taking any time to grieve herself. For the first time he found himself wondering if *this* was the real reason Neal had asked him to come.

'If you want to talk, I'm always happy to listen,' he said. Whatever she needed, wasn't that what he'd promised himself he was there for? Well, any idiot could see that she needed this.

'I don't know what to say.' Sadie gave a helpless little shrug. 'It's been two years… It seems too late. There was just so much to do. Taking care of Finn, the Azure, all the arrangements… He's buried back in England, near his family, you know? Of course you do. You were there, weren't you? At the funeral?'

'I was.'

'So it really is just me and Finn here.' She sounded like she might float away on a cloud of memories at any moment. Dylan tightened his hold on her shoulders, just enough to remind her to stay.

'And me,' he said.

'You're not permanent, though. You're like…in Monopoly. Just visiting.' She managed a small smile at the ridiculous joke, but he couldn't return it. There was no censure in the accusation, no bitterness at all. But that didn't change the way it stung.

Even if every word of it was true.

'I just don't know how to be everything Finn needs,' Sadie went on. 'Mother, father, his whole family… I don't know how to do that *and* save the Azure. But the hotel is Adem's legacy. It's the only part of him left here with us. So I have to. And I'm so scared that I'll fail.'

Her voice broke a little on the last word, and Dylan pulled her tighter to him. *Whatever she needs.*

'I'm here now,' he said. 'And I will come back, whenever you need me. Me, Neal, your parents, your sister… we're all here to help you. Whatever you need.'

It wasn't enough; he knew that even as he spoke the words. He wanted to promise he'd stay as long as she needed him. But he had a rule, a personal code, never to make promises he couldn't keep.

Everyone knew Dylan Jacobs couldn't do long term— him better than anyone.

'I'm here now,' he repeated, and wished that would be enough.

I'm here now.

Sadie burrowed deeper against the solid bulk of Dylan's shoulder, and ignored the fact that, even then, he couldn't bring himself to say he'd stay.

She was glad. He wasn't her boyfriend, her lover, wasn't anything more than a friend. She wasn't his responsibility. And even if she had been…it would have been a lie to say he'd stay, and they both knew it. Better to keep things honest.

She stared out at the scrubland before them and tried to ignore the sound of cars roaring past behind her. How could she have forgotten that driving to Ephesus would bring them this way? No, scrap that. She knew exactly how. Because all she'd been thinking about had been getting Dylan away from the hotel, fully clothed. Putting temptation out of reach before he fought past any more of her defences.

And yet here she was, clinging to him as if for her sanity, giving up all her secrets.

Maybe she should get some of his in return.

'Why do you hate the name of the Azure?' she asked, more for something else to focus on than any other reason. The fact that it probably led to a funny story with another woman—and a reminder why she couldn't become too reliant on him—was just a lucky bonus.

But Dylan said, 'My father walked out on us in another Azure Hotel. I was ten. We were there with him on some business trip. He just got into the car and drove away.'

'I'm sorry.' Sadie winced. Great way to lighten the mood.

Dylan shrugged, and she felt every muscle move against her cheek. 'It happens. He…he wasn't good at commitment. He stuck out family life as long as he could, then one day he just couldn't take it any more. I've never seen him since.'

'What did you do?' Sadie tried to imagine ten-year-old Dylan standing alone in the foyer of some strange hotel, but in her head the image morphed into two-year-old Finn, watching her cry as she tried to explain that Daddy wasn't coming home.

'I took my mum's purse and bought us three bus tickets back home—for me, Mum and my sister Cassie.'

'You became the man of the house.' She could see it so easily—Dylan just taking over and doing what was needed because there was no one else to do it. He'd been bogged down with commitment since the age of ten. No wonder he avoided it so thoroughly as an adult.

'I was all they had left. Mum didn't deal with it well.' From his tone Sadie could tell that was a huge understatement. 'By the time she could cope again I pretty much had it all in hand.'

Suddenly, a long-ago conversation came back to her. 'I remember Adem joking about all those dreadful part-time jobs you had at university. You were sending money home to your family?' Dylan nodded. 'That's why you shared that awful flat in London with Neal too, right?

Even after you were both earning enough to move somewhere nicer.'

All those puzzling facets of Dylan Jacobs that had never made sense fell into place to make a perfect diamond shape. A whole shine and side to him she'd never even considered.

'I'm like my dad in a lot of ways,' Dylan said, and Sadie frowned.

'Doesn't sound like it to me.'

'No, I am, and I know it.' He shrugged again. 'I've come to terms with it, too. I always want to be free to chase the next big thing, just like him. Difference is, I'd never let myself get tied down in the first place. I don't ever want to let anyone down the way he did.'

'You wouldn't,' Sadie said, knowing the truth of it in her bones.

'Anyway. He'd already abandoned my mum and sister. I couldn't do the same, so I took care of them however I could. Besides, they're not like you. They're hopeless on their own.'

'Oh?' Part of her felt warmed that he didn't consider her helpless and hopeless. But one small part of her brain wondered if he'd stay if he did. She stamped down on that part pretty quickly, before it could take hold.

'Yeah. My mum's on her third marriage, my sister's on her second. Every time something goes wrong I have to fly in and help pick up the pieces.' He shook his head. 'We *really* don't do commitment well in my family.'

Except for his commitment to them, which he seemed to hardly even recognise. 'I think commitment is something you have to practise every day,' she said. 'Every morning you have to make your commitment all over again or else it fades.'

'Maybe you're right.' He looked down at her, his expression thoughtful. 'I mean, you're the most committed person I know, so I guess you must be.'

'The most committed person you know? Is that meant to be a compliment?'

'Most definitely,' he assured her. 'Anyone else would have given up already, chucked in the towel and gone home. But not you. You committed to Adem and you won't let him down, even now he's gone. You're incredible.'

'Or possibly insane.' She shifted a little away, uncomfortable at his praise. Hadn't she let her husband down already, by being so distracted by fantasies of his best friend that she'd forgotten to even think about him today? Dylan being there confused her, made her forget to re-commit every morning. He made her think of other paths, other possibilities—just as he had twelve years before.

To Sadie, that felt like a pretty big betrayal in itself.

'There's always that possibility too,' Dylan said. 'But either way…I admire you, endlessly. You should know that.'

Sadie looked away, pushing her hands against the dirt ready to help herself stand.

'Ready to move?' Dylan jumped to his feet. 'We can still go back to the Azure…'

'I want to show you Ephesus,' Sadie said stubbornly. That was the plan after all.

'Fallen-down buildings it is, then.' He reached out a hand to pull her up and she took it tentatively. But once she was on her feet he pulled her close into a hug before she could let go. 'Sadie…your commitment—I meant what I said. It's admirable. But don't let it lock you into unhappiness either, okay? Adem would hate that.'

'I know.' The truth of his words trickled through her, fighting back against the guilt.

Dylan kissed her forehead, warm and comforting. 'Come on, then. Let's go and see some history.'

At least, Sadie thought as they got back in the car, this history belonged to other people. Her own was already too confusing.

CHAPTER TWELVE

SADIE SWUNG THE car into the dusty, rocky car park at Ephesus and smiled brightly at him, as if the scene at the roadside hadn't happened at all. Dylan was almost starting to doubt it had himself; it had been such a strange moment out of time when he had seemed to look deeper into the heart of Sadie than he ever had before.

That sort of revelation should have added some clarity to the situation, he felt. Instead, he was more confused than ever.

He hadn't meant to confess all his family's dark and depressing past to her, but somehow, with her sharing secrets, it had only seemed fair that he give back too. He'd tried to keep it as factual and unemotional as possible, knowing that the last thing she'd needed had been him falling apart too. She'd just needed to know that he'd understood, and that he cared. Hopefully he'd given her that.

But just reliving those moments had stirred up something in him he hadn't expected—something he'd barely had to deal with in years. The small boy left alone in charge of a family seemed so many light years away from where he was now that he never really drew a comparison day to day. He could almost forget the way the horror had slowly crept through him as he'd realised what had happened, and the searing pain that had followed, always when he'd least expected it, over the months to come, when it had struck home again what it had meant for his future.

Dylan shook his head. The moment had passed. No point dwelling any longer on things he couldn't even change twenty-odd years ago, let alone now.

They walked up through a street of stalls and cafés, selling hats and tourist tat, more scarves and costumes. Dylan ignored the sellers, but focussed in on the nearest café. Maybe something to eat and drink would do them good.

'Are you sure you want to do this now?' he asked. 'We could stop and grab a bite to eat before we go in.'

But Sadie was already striding ahead towards the ticket booths. By the time he caught up she had two tickets in her hand, ready to pass through the barriers.

Apparently, nothing was going to stop her today. Least of all him.

'Come on,' she said. 'There's masses to see, and we've already lost time.'

Dylan gave thanks for the bottled water and cereal bars in his backpack, and followed.

The path led them through scrubland littered with broken stones—some plain, some carved, all seriously less impressive than he suspected they would have been once. Information boards told them about the area, what had been here before Ephesus, and what had happened to the geography of the place.

'Did you know, there have been settlements in this area since six thousand BC?' Sadie asked.

'I didn't until I read that same information board.' Was she seriously going to talk history for the rest of the day? He supposed he could understand the need to put some distance between now and that heartbreaking conversation at the side of the road, but still. At some point they were going to have to return to the real world. 'Come on, I want to see the city proper.'

As they continued along the path, recognisable buildings started to appear—ruined and worn, but with walls and doorways and even decoration in places. Sadie stopped to read every single information board—often aloud—to him, despite the fact she must have been here plenty of times before. Dylan was sure it was all fascinating, but he had other things on his mind.

She'd admitted that she hadn't dealt with Adem's death, not really. He should have seen that sooner, or at least been more mindful of it. Was that why she was clinging so hard to the Azure?

And, if so, what would happen when she finally *did* deal with everything? Would she be ready to move on? Maybe even with him, for a time?

They turned off the path into an amphitheatre, and Sadie went skipping down the aisle steps to the stage, standing in the middle and calling out a line from some play or another, listening to the words reverberating around the stones.

Dylan took a seat on the carved steps, right up at the top, and watched her explore. Leaning back, he let the sun hit his face, the warmth soothe his body. Sadie wasn't the only one to have confessed all that morning, of course. He'd expected to feel shame or be pitied or something after telling her all about his family. But instead, next to her emotional outpouring, his ancient pains seemed like nothing. Still, somehow it felt good to have shared them. And it had helped Sadie too, he thought. She seemed lighter after her confessions that morning.

Maybe she really *was* ready to let go at last—not just saying the words to win his support and his money.

And if so…hopefully what he had planned for the night would help her make that leap.

The Library of Celsus might just be her favourite part of Ephesus, Sadie decided as she ran her fingers along the delicately carved stonework. It never ceased to amaze her, just imagining all the learning and history the place must have held once. One of the later buildings, from the Roman period, its magnificence had only lasted one hundred and forty-two years before an earthquake and ensuing fire had destroyed it, leaving only the façade—and even that had perished a couple of hundred years later, in another earthquake.

Strange to think that the beauty she stared at now had been rebuilt by modern hands; that they'd found a way to bring some life back to a pile of rubble. But they had. Maybe she could, too.

Turning, she saw Dylan standing at the bottom of the library steps, staring up at the columns and statues. Smiling, she trotted over to join him. She'd known that Ephesus would be just the distraction they needed—especially after that morning. No business, nothing personal—just ancient history.

'It's pretty incredible, isn't it?' Sadie moved to stand beside him, looking back at the façade again.

'It's certainly impressive,' Dylan agreed.

'So much history… A whole different world really.' Just where she wanted to be today.

Dylan turned to her, eyes obscured by his sunglasses. 'You know, I don't remember you being so much of a history buff when we were younger.'

Sadie shrugged. 'Maybe I wasn't, back when the history around me was so familiar. But here…the history here blows me away. I want to know all of it.'

'Why?' Dylan asked, and she frowned at him. She should have known Mr Next Big Thing wouldn't get the appeal of bygone days. 'No, seriously, I'm curious. Why does it matter so much to you?'

'I guess because…well, it shows us where we came from. Where we've been and how far there still is to go. There's a lot of lessons in history.'

'Perhaps.' Dylan looked away, back at the library again. 'But I'm not so sure it can tell us what happens next.'

'You've never heard of history repeating itself?' she asked.

'Of course. But I like to think that we're more than just the sum of what has happened to us.'

Sadie followed his gaze back to the library façade. Suddenly she could see the cracks, the places it had been repaired, and where parts were still missing, in a way she never had before.

She was also pretty sure they weren't talking about the Ancient Greeks and Romans any more.

Was he right? Were they more than their history?

How could he say that when everything he'd told her that morning—about his dad, his family—had so clearly formed him into exactly the sort of man he was? Of course he didn't believe he could do commitment, coming from a family like that. It had even explained to her why he was so desperate not to miss chances—how many opportunities must he have given up to look after his mother and sister? It was a miracle he'd ever made it to university to meet Adem in the first place.

'Come on,' Dylan said, tugging on her arm. 'Let's keep going or we'll never see everything.'

Side by side, they climbed the paved hill through more terraces and temples and half-reassembled mosaics through the rest of the town.

'I mean, look at the people who lived here,' Dylan said suddenly, and Sadie frowned, trying to cast her mind back to the conversation they'd been having.

'What do you mean?'

'Well, they built this fantastic city, survived invasions and slaughters, were Greek, Roman, Byzantine...then the river silted up, the earthquakes hit, and the place started falling apart. And I bet you they never saw it coming—even though it had all happened before—however well they knew their own history.'

'I guess there are always twists and turns we can't predict,' Sadie admitted. 'And maybe sometimes we just choose to hope for the best instead.' Like she had, hoping for a long, happy life with her husband.

'You know that better than most, huh?' He gave her an apologetic half-smile, even though he hadn't done anything wrong, not really. She just wasn't meant to live happily ever after, it seemed. Not his fault. 'It's just kind of sad to think of all those people watching the harbour silt up, losing their access to the Aegean—the only thing that made this place matter—and realising there was nothing to stay for any more.'

Nothing to stay for... The words pricked at her mind, and she knew she'd been right, back at the library, to think they weren't really talking history any more.

'Is this some convoluted way of telling me that you think my harbour is silting up?' she asked sharply, stopping in the middle of the path and not even caring about the tourists behind who had to swerve suddenly. The anger bubbling up as she reran his words in her head mattered more.

Dylan glanced back at her and stopped walking himself. 'Your harbour?' he asked, voice laced with confusion.

'The Azure,' Sadie snapped. As if he didn't know what she was talking about. 'Look, just lose the metaphor. If you think there's no future for my hotel, that it can't be saved, tell me now.'

'You're wrong.' Dylan shook his head.

'Am I really?' Folding her arms across her chest, Sadie tapped one foot against the ancient stones and waited for him to deny it again.

If he dared.

Had the woman actually lost her mind this time?

Dylan grabbed Sadie's arm and pulled her away from the middle of the path into the shade of a gnarled old tree beside a tumbledown wall. Maybe the heat was getting to her. He fished in his bag for a bottle of water and handed it to her.

'Drink some of this,' he said, sighing when she managed to do so without breaking her glare at him. 'Look, I believe the Azure can be saved, okay? I'm just not sure that you're the person to do it.'

She lowered the bottle from her lips, her expression crestfallen. 'You don't think I can do it.'

He bit back a curse. That was not what he'd meant. God, how many ways could he mess this up? 'I'm very sure that you can. But I'm still not convinced that you really want to.'

'We're back to this?' She shoved the bottle back into his hands and cool droplets dribbled out onto his fingers. 'I've given you a million reasons—'

'And none of them are "because it's the work I know I was born to do".'

'Who has that? No one, Dylan. No one else expects that from their job.'

'You should.' He took a long drink of water. 'The difference between you and most people is that this isn't your only option. And obligation isn't passion, Sadie.'

'Fine.' She shook her head, stepping away from him. The extra distance felt like miles instead of inches. 'If this is too big a project for you, too big a commitment, just say so. I'll find some other way to save the Azure.'

She would too, he knew. Sighing, he rubbed a fist across his tired eyes. How had a simple sightseeing trip grown so complicated?

'I know things have been weird between us this week.' Her tone was softer now, and it only made him more nervous. 'But I swear I'm not asking for anything beyond your business and financial support, if that's what you're worried about. I...I think that maybe there could be something between us, yes. But I'm not trying to tie you down, or drag you away from your other opportunities.'

Something between us... Wasn't that the understatement of the year?

'I never thought you were.' At least he hadn't. Until she'd said that.

'Well...good.' She shifted awkwardly from one foot to the other, and he was pretty sure the faint pink flush on her cheeks wasn't just to do with the sun. 'So. Are you in, or not?'

She wanted an answer now. After days of dancing around everything between them—history, business, attraction—suddenly she needed to know. Of course she did.

'Can we discuss this at dinner?' he asked. If he'd read things right, tonight would be the perfect time to present his whole proposal in one go. A chance for them to maybe think about the future for once, instead of the past.

And he reckoned the odds on her saying yes were much better there than here at the side of the road through an abandoned city.

But Sadie stood her ground. 'No. I need to know now. Will you recommend investing in the Azure to your board?'

When had she got so stubborn? Or had she always been this way? Was it one of the things Adem had loved about her? He could hardly remember. The Sadie that had been had almost entirely given way to the new one, the one he'd spent the last week falling for.

He took a deep breath and dived in.

'I have a proposal for you,' he said, wishing his heart wasn't beating so loudly.

'Another one?'

'Yes. I'll help you save the Azure, if that's what you really want.'

'It is.' The words came fast enough, but did he hear a flicker of doubt behind them?

'You might want to wait and hear me out before you make that decision.'

She shook her head. 'I'm sure.'

'Really? Because I think you want something more. And I can give that to you.' He could see her considering it, the temptation on her face clear.

'What?' she finally asked, a little grudgingly.

And here they were. His one chance to win her away from this place. 'I recently took over a chain of hotels—mostly in the UK. I want to turn them into luxury spa hotels—and I think you'd be the person to help develop the spa aspect of them.'

Temptation gave way to shock as her eyebrows rose, frozen high on her forehead. 'I don't… I don't know what to say.'

Which meant she was considering it, right? Time to press the advantage.

'You'd be home in Britain, with your family,' he said, knowing he was sweetening the deal with every word. He'd spent enough time with her that week that he knew what she wanted—even if she wouldn't admit it. 'Finn would have your parents close too. You'd have support, help—and a generous, regular salary. If you really wanted, we could bring the Azure under the chain umbrella, put a new manager in charge…but it would still be yours and Finn's.' He had no idea how that would even work, or what his lawyers would say about it, but he'd say anything to get her to take the deal.

To have a reason to keep her close, to see her regularly, to have her in his life. However he could get her.

But it was more than that, he insisted silently. It was the right thing for her, too. And an opportunity most people would bite his hand off for.

Not Sadie, though. She still looked torn.

'Just think about it,' he said, and she nodded absently, her lower lip caught between her teeth.

He couldn't resist. The timing was wrong, nothing was as he had planned, they still had business to resolve, but he had to kiss her now. Before he went insane with wanting it.

CHAPTER THIRTEEN

SHE KNEW WHAT he was going to do a split second before
he moved, could see it in his eyes, the way they softened
and warmed. And, just like last time, Sadie knew she
should pull away, back off, escape.

Except she didn't.

His hand came up to her waist and she let it, drawing
a breath that burned her lungs at the touch. And when
he dipped his head, she raised her chin to meet him, her
lips aligning perfectly with his, as if they were meant
to be kissed.

As if she'd been waiting her whole life for this.

Had that small, contented noise really come from
her mouth? From the way Dylan wrapped his other arm
around her, hauling her tight against his body as he deep-
ened the kiss, she suspected it had. And she knew, without a shadow of a doubt, that their whole week together
had been building up to this. She didn't know if it was
history repeating itself, or the future imposing on her de-
termination to cling onto the past, but this, this moment,
this kiss, had always been inevitable.

It was what followed that was completely unclear.

After long, long, perfect moments Dylan pulled back,
just enough to allow air between their lips again. His
face was still so close that she could see every fleck of

colour in his eyes, every hint of worry in his expression. He didn't know what happened next either, and somehow that made her feel a little better.

'So you'll think about it?' Dylan cleared his throat. 'My business proposal, I mean.'

Her eyes fluttering closed, Sadie let out a low laugh. All business, this man. 'Yes. I'll think about it.'

His hands dropped from her waist and she stepped back, sucking in the air that seemed to have disappeared for the length of their kiss.

'We should get back,' Dylan said. 'I have something great planned for tonight, and you're not going to want to miss it.'

Something more spectacular than that kiss? Sadie doubted it. 'There's not much more to see anyway. Just the gift shop. If you think you can live without a magnetic Library of Celsus…'

'I don't think I need anything more to remember this day by,' Dylan said, his gaze fixed on hers. 'I won't be forgetting our time in Ephesus in a hurry.'

'Neither will I,' Sadie admitted.

They made their way slowly back down the hill, inches separating them. Sadie wondered if she should be holding his hand—back when she'd last kissed someone for the first time, that had been the sort of thing you did afterwards. But, then, Dylan had never struck her as a handholding type.

She had too much to think about to make conversation on the drive back to the Azure, or do more than clench her jaw a little tighter when they passed the spot where they'd stopped earlier. Dylan's offer, for one, quite apart from that heartstopping kiss.

Why was he offering her this now? He'd come here to help bail out the Azure, but now it seemed he had other plans entirely. And as much as she appreciated him think-ing of her…she couldn't help but wonder if this was just his way of keeping her close without actually having to commit to her in any way.

It was a stupid thought. They'd shared one kiss, that was all. But if they did decide to take things further… what happened next? What *could* happen, when Dylan had made it very clear that he wasn't the sort of man who stuck around?

Maybe she needed to separate the business from the personal—except that was impossible when her late hus-band's legacy *was* her business, and his best friend's job offer might just be a coded message for, 'Let's be friends with benefits.'

No, that wasn't fair. Whatever there was between her and Dylan, it was more than that, she could feel it. What was between them *mattered.*

But not enough for him to change his whole life phi-losophy—if she even wanted him to.

She sighed. If she took the job, it would mean aban-doning her commitments here. And even if it was what she wanted to do, was it worth the risk to her heart? Dylan Jacobs had held a tiny corner of it for a very long time, she finally admitted to herself, and if she let him take more…well, she might not get it back.

And that was a big risk to take, for anyone.

'You okay?' Dylan asked.

She nodded, then realised she was already parked out-side the Azure. When had that happened?

'What's the plan for tonight?' she asked unenthusiasti-cally. She needed a long bath and an early night to think about her options, but it was Dylan's last night.

He flashed her an enigmatic smile as he climbed out of the car. 'Just meet me in the lobby at eight. It's a surprise.'

Just what she needed. More unexpected things happening in her life. 'Can you at least tell me what I should wear?'

'Anything you like.' He leaned back inside the car and pressed a swift kiss to her lips. 'You always look beautiful to me.'

And then he was gone, skipping up the steps to the Azure Hotel and leaving Sadie feeling more confused than ever.

Dylan refused to pace the lobby this time. The car was waiting outside, he was suited and booted in his best dinner suit and a crisp, new white shirt. Everything was going to be perfect.

As soon as Sadie showed up.

She didn't keep him waiting too long. He turned as the elevator let out its familiar ping and watched breathlessly as the doors opened and Sadie stepped out.

'Wow.' He'd been aiming for something more eloquent, but from the pink that hit her cheeks, honesty worked just as well. 'You look spectacular.'

'Thanks.' She looked down at her red cocktail dress and swirled her hips a little, making it rise and fall. The movement made every muscle in Dylan's body tighten.

If he didn't know better, he'd say that Sadie had plans for tonight, too.

'I've been saving it for a special occasion,' she said, taking his arm as they walked out of the hotel together. 'I thought that tonight might fit the bill.'

'I hope so.' Now that he was close enough he could feel the slight tremor in her hands, hear the tiny wobble in her voice. Dress aside, she wasn't as confident as she was making out. It made him feel a little better, actually—

because his confidence was giving way to nerves by the second.

'I, uh, I emailed you the proposal. For the Azure, I mean.' Had she? He hadn't checked. And that in itself told him that his priorities were shifting. 'We could look through it later tonight, if you wanted…'

Dylan shook his head. 'It can wait until tomorrow.' Tonight couldn't be about business, he could sense that. It needed to be about them. But the two were so closely linked…would they really be able to untangle them?

The car he'd hired sped them down to the marina, and he tipped the driver generously when they got out. If everything went to plan, they wouldn't need him until the next morning.

'The marina?' Sadie asked, looking around her at the lights. The whole town seemed lit up in the almost darkness of the autumn evening. 'What are we doing here?'

'I have a friend who has a yacht—and he owed me a favour,' Dylan explained, leading her towards the vessel in question. 'So tonight we shall be dining aboard the *Marie Bell*, catered by one of the finest chefs I've ever met. And, if it's okay with you, I thought we might take her out for a spin out on the Aegean.'

Her gaze shot to his. 'Overnight?'

'Yes. She has two bedrooms, and is fully equipped with anything we might need for an overnight stay, but if you'd rather come back sooner…' He trailed off. 'This can be anything you want, Sadie. I just wanted to give you a special night.'

She nodded slowly, her teeth tugging on her lower lip again in that way that just made him mad to kiss her. 'Okay.'

The yacht was every bit as spectacular as his friend had described, and watching Sadie stand at the prow as they motored out of the marina, staring out at the dark-ening water, Dylan knew he'd made a good choice in bringing her there. They needed tonight—even if it was all they ever got.

And just in case it was, he intended to make the most of every single moment.

Grabbing a bottle of champagne and two glasses from the bar, he headed out on deck to share it with Sadie.

Sadie stared out at the water, dark and constantly chang-ing under the moonlight. Dinner had been beautiful— all four courses of it—and more than made up for their skipped lunch at Ephesus. The conversation, too, had been light and easy—after Dylan had declared a morato-rium on business talk the moment they'd sat down. And neither of them had seemed inclined to discuss the past after the day they'd spent together.

Instead, they'd talked about Finn, about cities Dylan had visited recently, places she'd love to go one day, her sister and parents—anything except what was happen-ing between them, or anything that mattered.

It almost felt like a first date.

But now dinner was over and she had to decide what came next. She could tell Dylan was leaving it up to her— which was probably why he'd removed all their other is-sues from the evening.

It was just them now.

No hotel, no history—no husband. Not any more.

She shivered, and Dylan wrapped his jacket around her shoulders without a word.

Out here at sea, it was just Sadie and Dylan. And it was up to her to decide what that meant.

But only for tonight.

That, she was sure, was the main reason he'd brought

her so far from the real world. Not just to give her a treat at the end of his visit but because, whatever she decided, once they returned to shore it was all over. He'd move on. They'd be business partners perhaps, or maybe not. She hoped they'd still be friends, whatever happened.

But nothing more.

'You're thinking too hard.' Dylan rested against the rail beside her, leaning back to get a good look at her. The lights from the boat lit his face, but hers must be hidden in shadow, she assumed. Yet still he stared at it. 'You're supposed to be relaxing.'

Sadie turned, her back to the water, and he shifted nearer, until he was half in front of her, so close against her right side that she could feel his muscles against her body, even through two layers of clothes.

No pretending this was anything other than it was now. And not even a hint of a suggestion that they might be using that second bedroom.

Sadie sucked in a breath, the scent of him mixed with the sea air filling her lungs, an intoxicating combination. God, she wanted him so much. It felt good to admit that, after so long.

Maybe she always had. But want and love were very different things—and she'd loved Adem.

Strangely, it was that thought that made it all feel possible. This wasn't love—and never would or could be with a man like Dylan. For him, love was commitment and thus impossible. However he felt about her, he'd never let it move past tonight—so neither would she.

Sleeping with him wasn't the same as betraying Adem's memory, not in the way she'd been afraid it would be. Not unless she never planned to sleep with another man again for the rest of her life. At thirty-two, that seemed a little impractical, even to her.

She could have this. She could have one night and no more. She could give in to that curious want that had plagued her since she'd met this man—and that had only worsened over the last week.

As long as she walked away with her heart intact in the morning. And her heart was buried in England with her husband.

Decision made, Sadie rose up on tiptoe before she could change her mind. Dylan's eyes widened, just a fraction, and his arms tightened around her. But he didn't move closer. He was still leaving this up to her.

Sadie closed her eyes, raised her lips to his, and took what she wanted.

The first kiss was gentle, tentative, like the one in Ephesus. But within moments it changed.

'God, Sadie,' Dylan muttered against her lips, and his arms hauled her up against his body so her bottom rested on the higher rail and she could barely touch the deck with her toes. It should have felt unsafe but with Dylan's arms so tight around her body she knew there was no chance of her falling.

She knew he'd never let her go.

'I can't tell you how long I've waited for this,' he murmured, as she placed kisses across his jaw and down his throat.

'About as long as I have,' she admitted, pressing an extra kiss to the hollow of his collar bone, as thanks for discarding his tie and undoing those top shirt buttons after dinner.

His thigh pressed between her legs, her bright red dress rising up high above her knees, and the pressure almost made her lose her mind.

'Really?' he asked, dipping his head for another kiss. 'You wanted this too?'

'Always,' she admitted. 'I just never thought I could have it.' Or should.

'Because— No. Not tonight.' He kissed her firmly. 'Tonight is just for us. No ghosts, no history, nothing between us.'

Sadie looked up into his eyes, almost black with wanting her, and kissed him in agreement. 'Just us. Just for tonight.' She swallowed, hunting down that last bit of courage she needed. 'So, how about you show me the bedroom you promised me this place had?'

Dylan grinned, a wolfish look on his face. God, what was she letting herself in for? And how would anything after it ever live up to tonight?

'Your wish is my command,' he said, and Sadie knew none of it mattered.

Just for tonight she was going to live in the moment, and enjoy every second of it.

CHAPTER FOURTEEN

DYLAN WOKE TO the feeling of something missing. Forcing his tired eyes to open, he waited for them to focus then frowned at the sight of Sadie already pulling that glorious red dress over her even more spectacular body. Without looking back at the bed, she began hunting around for her shoes, pulling them on as she found them.

Huh. Talk about a rude awakening.

Last night had been everything he'd ever dreamt it might be, and more. He could never have imagined the way they moved together would be so in tune, so perfect. He didn't know what had changed that week but, whatever it was, it had only brought the two of them more in sync.

But apparently that perfect connection was over with the sunrise.

'Morning,' he said, levering himself into a seated position and letting the sheets fall away from his torso.

Sadie jumped at the sound of his voice, which gave him some small satisfaction. 'You're awake.'

'As are you. And dressed, too.'

'Yeah, well…we're back in the marina,' she said. He wanted her to come and sit beside him on the bed, just enjoy these last few moments away from the real world, but the look on her face stopped him short of suggesting it. What was it he saw there? Uncertainty, a hint of fear, maybe a little sadness? Or was he just projecting his own feelings onto her expression?

'Time to get back to the real world, then, huh?'

'I guess so.'

'You should have woken me,' he said, trying to inject lightness into the words, to try and break the strange new tension in the room. 'Before you put all those pesky clothes back on, for preference.'

'I suppose you're usually the one slipping out of a borrowed room the morning after, huh?' Her smile suggested it was meant to be a joke, but the words fell flat between them as Dylan felt his mood worsening.

'You were slipping out on me?'

'No!' Sadie said, too fast. 'I mean, it's not like you wouldn't know where to find me, right?'

Was that the only reason? God, what had happened in her head between him falling asleep boneless and sated and the moment he'd woken up this morning? Dylan had no idea—and he wasn't sure he was going to be allowed to find out.

'So it's back to the Azure, then,' he said. Apparently their moratorium on business was over, too. 'That's what happens next?'

'I think it has to be,' Sadie said. 'I mean, you have a flight to catch this afternoon, and you still haven't checked over the Azure proposal. I think I included everything we've talked about, but if you have any questions it would be good to deal with them sooner rather than later. I'm leaving for England in a couple of days to fetch Finn home, remember.'

Home. So Turkey was still home to her. Good to know.

Dylan reached for his pants. Talking business naked just felt wrong. 'Never mind the Azure proposal right now. Have you thought any more about my proposition?'

he asked, wishing the moment the sentence was out that he'd chosen any word other than 'proposition'.

'I...I'm not sure it would be the best idea.'

'Because of last night?'

'Because of lots of things.' She bit her lower lip, and Dylan had to sit on his hands to stop himself reaching for her and kissing them back to last night again. 'Will you still present the Azure proposal to your board for investment? Even if I'm still in charge?'

'Of course,' he said, the words almost sticking in his throat. 'You've certainly demonstrated the potential of Kuşadası and even the hotel itself as a viable investment. I'll talk to them as soon as I get back.'

'Great. Thanks.'

Awkward silence stretched between them until Dylan thought he might snap. Grabbing his shirt from the floor, he tossed it over his shoulders before striding across the luxurious cabin towards the bathroom. 'Why don't you go see if you can go scare us up some breakfast?' he suggested over his shoulder. 'I'll be there in a few minutes.'

If it was back to business as usual, he needed a shower, some food and plenty of coffee. Hopefully one of those would fill the yawning gap that seemed to have opened up in his chest.

Sadie kept it together until they reached the hotel, a feat she was rather proud of. It would have been so easy, that morning, to turn over and back into Dylan's arms. To let their one perfect night stretch just a little further. But it would have only prolonged the agony.

Because for all her arguments to herself the night before she had no doubt that letting him go again was going to be excruciatingly painful.

How was she supposed to go back to business, or even to being friends, now that she knew how it felt to have his skin against hers, his body pressing hers down into the bed with glorious pleasure? How was she supposed to even *think* about anything else?

But she had to. Because no matter how miffed he might have looked at being upstaged in the casual morning-after stakes, Dylan didn't want anything else. Oh, he might convince himself that they could be something more—but it wouldn't be a commitment, not from him. He wasn't Adem, and she had to remember that. Keep it at the front of her mind at all times.

Or else she had a horrible feeling she could slide so easily into love with the man.

And that *would* be a betrayal. Maybe not of her wedding vows—she knew that if Adem had lived she would never have taken this step, never have had this chance to explore what could be between her and Dylan—and not even of her husband's memory, not really. Rachel had been right in that at least—Adem would rather see her happy than alone.

But she'd be betraying herself. Betraying what she wanted—no, needed—from her own future. Maybe Dylan had been right when he'd said the Azure wasn't her dream, but he couldn't see that it was a part of something bigger. A chance for her to live her life with her son—and she didn't want that life to be confused and clouded by a man who came, made them love him, but never stayed. She wouldn't do that to Finn—or to herself.

Maybe Dylan would change one day, find something or someone worth committing to. But she couldn't take the chance that the thing or person he found might be her. Not when it would affect Finn too.

And it would, she knew. Her own fluctuating emotions

after one week, one night told her that. She needed to be solid and steady for her son, and Dylan Jacobs made her the opposite of both.

'I'd better pack,' Dylan said, as they stood in the lobby of the Azure, more than a metre of marble floor between them.

Sadie nodded her agreement. 'Your car will be here at two. I'll come down and see you off.'

'You don't have to.' He sounded so distant Sadie had to swallow a large lump in her throat before she could answer.

'Yes, I do.'

'Fine. I'll see you then.' He strode off towards the lifts, without looking back.

Sadie took a deep breath and went to check in with the front desk for any important news or messages, hoping they wouldn't comment on how overdressed she was for the task.

Then she was going up to her room to take a bath and break down in private.

The second hand ticked around the clock face seemingly slower than ever, but still inexorably working its way towards two o'clock. Sadie smoothed down her black suit one more time and tucked her still-damp hair behind her ears. At least the make-up seemed to be holding strong— her eyes weren't nearly as blotchy as they'd been a quarter of an hour ago.

In—she checked the clock again—twelve minutes' time she'd go down to the lobby. That, assuming Dylan arrived early too, would give her ten whole minutes to say goodbye to him.

It wasn't enough, but Sadie was starting to worry that no amount of time would be. She'd been so focussed on the fact that he'd be walking away the next day she hadn't spent enough time considering the fact that she wouldn't be able to—not from the memories and not from her feelings.

Dylan might not be the committing sort, but she was—and she should have remembered that before she'd fallen into bed with him. She'd never been the one-night stand sort, so why on earth had she thought she could start now?

She sighed, and sat back down on the bed. Because she'd wanted it so badly, that was why. She'd wanted that one night—and now she'd had it she couldn't give it back. And, truth be told, she wasn't sure she even wanted to.

A sudden hammering on the door jerked her out of her thoughts. Blinking—and hoping the waterproof mascara was still holding up—she quickly crossed the floor and opened the door.

'Dylan.' She was supposed to have another eleven minutes before she had to face him. What unfairness was this?

Without a word he pushed past her into the room. Sadie shut the door behind her; from the furious expression on his face she had a feeling this conversation wasn't one she wanted to share with the rest of the hotel.

'Okay, I'm leaving in, like, fifteen minutes, but I need to know something first.' He had his hands in his pockets, but from the look of the material they were bunched into fists. 'What happens next?'

'Next?' Sadie gulped. The question she'd been avoiding. 'Well, like we said, it's back to business. We can be business partners, hopefully, and friends for definite. I hope Finn and I will be seeing more of you in the future.' Even if it tore at her heart every time. Dylan was part of Adem's life too, and Finn deserved the chance to know him. She just needed to make sure she guarded her emotions more carefully—something that would certainly be easier with her son present.

'So last night was…?'

'Wonderful,' she admitted, with a small smile. 'But I told you, I never expected anything more. I'm not trying to tie you down or make you commit to anything. Well, anything more than saving my hotel.'

'You make it sound like everything that has happened between us this week was only about you getting my investment.'

'You know that's not true,' Sadie admonished. Whatever he might think of her today, he had to know she wasn't the money-grabbing woman his words suggested.

'Do I?' he asked, one eyebrow raised.

'I bloody well hope so!' Her own temper started to heat and rise to match his. Ten more minutes and they could have avoided this completely, parted civilly. But, no, he had to storm in here and demand the last say, didn't he?

'In that case, I can only assume that you slept with me as some sort of personal experiment,' Dylan said, the words sharp. 'A chance to find out what you could have had. And now you're burying yourself back in your old life, the tired old plan that wasn't working.'

'Sounds to me like you don't like being treated the way you've treated God knows how many women over the years,' Sadie bit back. 'What, it's okay for you to indulge in one night and call it quits, but God forbid a woman tries to do the same to you.'

'That's not what this was!' Dylan yelled. 'What we had—'

'Was a mutual attraction we worked out of our systems last night.' The lie hurt even to speak it, but what other option was there? Ask for more and watch Dylan flounder when he realised he couldn't offer it? She might have hurt his manly pride, but that had to be better than letting him destroy any self-respect she had left.

'It was more than that, and you know it.' His tone was low now, dangerous, daring Sadie to deny it.

She couldn't.

'Even if it was,' she said softly, 'it was never going to be anything more than this week, and it's not fair of you to pretend that it was. I have Finn and the Azure to think about, and you have your business… You're leaving any minute now, for heaven's sake.'

'But I'll come back. I said I'd come back.' He made it sound like a huge commitment. Probably because he had no idea what a real one looked or sounded like.

'And there'll always be a friendly welcome for you here.'

'Friends.' He barked a harsh laugh. 'You really think we can go back to that?'

'I think we have to,' Sadie said pragmatically. 'Because, Dylan, you can't offer me anything else.'

'I offered you a new career. A chance to start over.'

'What I want most is the chance to have a future with my son.' The truth, if not quite all of it.

'And what about me? Are you really going to let your dead husband and this bloody hotel stop you from moving on and being happy?'

She could have laughed at the cruel irony of it. Here he was, the ultimate playboy, asking for more—and she couldn't give it to him, however much she wanted to. Because he didn't even know what it meant.

'Are you honestly telling me you're ready to become a father—to a little boy you've barely met?' The sudden shock on his face was answer enough. 'Exactly. Dylan, you're not Adem, and I never expected you to be. I went into this with my eyes open. But you don't do commitment and I need that in my life—for Finn, as well as myself. We need stability and certainty more than ever now. And you can't give us that.'

You're not Adem.

Wasn't that what it always came down to? In the end, it wouldn't have mattered who'd met her first, who'd loved her most, who could give her what—he wasn't Adem. So he was always going to lose.

'I'm not even second choice to you, am I?' he murmured, watching her eyes widen. Could she sense the fury building inside him? He hoped so. But he also knew he needed to get out of there before it exploded. He'd never hurt her, but if they wanted to remain even business acquaintances there were some things they couldn't come back from. 'I'm no choice at all.'

'Finn is my choice,' Sadie said, but he knew what she meant. She would always choose Adem—even his memory—over moving on with him. Over giving him a chance to see if maybe, just maybe, this time he could stick at something. 'Yours is the next big thing. It always has been, and it always will be. You know that, Dylan.'

'Just like my old man, huh?' He knew it himself, always had. But it still hurt to hear it from her—the one woman he'd thought, for a moment, that he could be something more for. Someone better.

'That's not what—' Sadie started.

'Yes,' he replied. 'You did.'

So, really, what was there left to say?

'My assistant will be in touch about the investment proposal in due course,' he said. 'I'm sure it will go through without a problem.'

Sadie nodded but didn't speak. He supposed she'd got

the only thing she wanted anyway. At least one of them was ending this week happy.

'Goodbye, Sadie.' He turned on his heel and walked out, hoping his car was already waiting downstairs.

He didn't let himself believe that the sound he heard behind him as he shut the door was a sob.

CHAPTER FIFTEEN

SADIE DROPPED HER suitcase onto the spare bed in her parents' back bedroom and began rummaging through it for a cardigan. England might be colder than she'd remembered, but it was still good to be home, however temporarily.

Anything was better than moping around the Azure Hotel alone.

At least she had Finn back now. Once they headed home to Turkey, it would be the two of them against the world again, and everything would be fine. Just one look at his beaming face as he'd waved his 'Mummy' sign, surrounded by pictures of aircraft, when she'd arrived at the airport had told her that she'd done the right thing. When he'd wrapped his little arms around her neck and hugged her tight she'd known there was no other choice she could have made.

Finn was the only thing that mattered now. All she had left.

'Knock-knock.' Her sister Rachel appeared in the open doorway, both hands occupied with cups of tea. 'Mum thought you might need this after your journey.'

'Definitely.' Family, a cup of tea, familiar surroundings…this was all exactly what she needed.

A whoop of excitement from outside caught her attention and she moved to the window, cup of tea in hand. In the back garden Finn and his cousins appeared to be playing some sort of game involving a football, three hula-hoops and a garden chair. Whatever the rules, he seemed to be having fun, even wrapped up in his coat and scarf instead of still being in tee shirt and shorts, as he would have been in Turkey.

'The kids have loved having Finn here to play with,' Rachel said, following her gaze. 'It's been lovely for them to all have some time together.'

'I know.' A flicker of guilt at keeping Finn so far away from his family ran through her. 'And I know Adem's parents enjoyed having him for a sleepover last weekend.' More people they didn't see enough of.

'I bet. It must be even harder for them.'

'They came out to visit in the spring,' Sadie said defensively.

'Not the same as having him round the corner, though, is it?'

No, it wasn't. Sadie sank to sit on the edge of the bed and blew across the top of her tea to cool it. 'Finn asked me if we really had to go back to Turkey,' she admitted. 'He's loved being here so much.'

Rachel winced as she sat beside her. 'Sorry. Didn't mean to make things worse.'

'It's the truth, though, isn't it?'

'But not all of it. If you're truly happy out in Turkey then Finn will be too. You know kids, they're always happiest exactly where they are, never ready to move on to the next thing. Especially if it's bedtime.'

The exact opposite of Dylan. Sadie huffed a tiny laugh into her mug at the thought.

'How are things at the Azure anyway?' Rachel asked.

'Any luck with the investment guy—personal or professional?' She nudged Sadie gently in the ribs.

'Dylan's going to present my proposal to the board, but he thinks they should go for investing.' There. She'd said his name without crying. A definite improvement. And the proposal was good—she'd worked on it with Neal before Dylan's arrival for weeks, and had tweaked it to fit everything she and Dylan had talked about on his visit. It was just what he'd wanted, she hoped.

'And personally?' Rachel pressed. 'Come on, Sade. I saw you all dressed up for him, remember? There was definitely something going on there.'

'Well, if there was, it was for one night only,' Sadie said.

Rachel frowned. 'That idiot walked out on you after one night?'

'Yeah. Well, no. I...I guess I walked out on him.'

'That doesn't sound much like you.'

'It was a pre-emptive strike,' Sadie explained. 'He doesn't do commitment, and it was more important to me that we stay friends and business partners. Apart from anything else, Finn doesn't need any more uncertainty in his life.'

'And how's that working out for you?' Rachel asked doubtfully.

'It's fine,' Sadie lied. 'It's for the best.' She just had to keep telling herself that. And not acknowledge the secret fear that kept her awake at night—that she had gone and fallen head first in love with Dylan Jacobs.

Even she couldn't be that stupid, right?

'He did offer me a different business proposal, though,' she said. Better to get the conversation back on professional terms. 'It would mean working back here in the UK, putting a manager in charge at the Azure.'

'That would be perfect!' Rachel bounced a little on the mattress. 'You and Finn could come home and still keep the Azure! Have you told Mum and Dad yet?'

'I turned him down,' Sadie admitted, with a wince.

Rachel stopped bouncing. 'Because you slept with him?'

'Because…it didn't feel right.' Of course, nothing had felt right since Dylan had left either. But how much harder would this be if she had to see him all the time for work, too? No, much better this way, with her safely tucked away in Turkey and him travelling the world, popping in for the occasional friendly visit. Knowing Dylan, they'd be lucky to see him more than once a year.

Another depressing thought.

'Well, I suppose you know best,' Rachel said, although her tone clearly said otherwise.

'I hope so,' Sadie whispered.

Otherwise it was entirely possible she'd made the biggest mistake of her life, sending Dylan away.

'Well, you're in a foul mood,' Dylan's sister Cassie said. He dropped into the wooden chair beside her, exhausted after an hour or more racing around the scrubland that surrounded her home with her two boys.

'Hey, you should be nicer to the guy who's been keeping up with your two tearaways for the past week.' Not that it was a chore particularly. Keeping two six-and nine-year-old boys entertained took energy and concentration, and worked marvellously as a distraction. Of course, it helped that it was also fun.

Much more fun than dwelling on how things had ended with Sadie anyway.

Cassie handed him a cold beer and he took it gratefully. 'Want to tell me about it?'

'I don't know what you're talking about,' Dylan lied.

'Seriously?' Raising her eyebrows at him, Cassie put her own bottle down and ticked her observations off on her fingers. 'First, you arrive here with no warning. You drag the boys off to play outside whenever they ask you questions about your travels. You haven't been to see Mum, even though you've been here for days. And, most importantly, you've almost drunk all my beer.'

'I'll buy you more beer.'

'That's not the point.' Cassie sighed. 'Go on, I'm listening. Detail your boring work problem and I'll make the necessary sympathetic noises as needed. Unless it isn't work…' She sat up straighter. 'In which case I might be much more interested.'

'It's nothing.' Dylan took a swig of his beer, glad it was a million miles away from the local wine he'd drunk with Sadie in Turkey. The fewer reminders the better right now. He'd spoken to the board, had got them to approve the investment and had handed the whole mess over to his assistant before he'd left for his sister's place in Sydney. He just wanted to move on.

'Which means it's a woman,' Cassie guessed. 'Okay, let me see… She's married to someone else? Or just not interested. Oh, Dylan, did you finally find a woman who *doesn't* want you?'

'Not exactly.' Although, really, wasn't that the truth? Sure, she'd wanted him for one night, but that had been it.

Dylan sent up a silent apology to every woman he'd ever spent just one night with, even if he'd been upfront about it from the start. Being on the opposite end showed him exactly how much it sucked.

'So what happened?' Cassie pulled her feet up under her on her chair, just like she'd done when she'd been little. 'You've got me all curious now. Don't leave me hanging.'

Dylan sighed. Cassie had always been stubborn. There was no way he was getting out of this conversation without giving up at least the basic facts.

'I went to Turkey to see an old friend, to see if I could help her business out. We…connected in a way we hadn't before, that's all.' He shrugged. No big deal, no drama, no hole in his chest filled with a swirling vacuum of rage and confusion and disappointment. Nothing to see at all.

'That's all?' Cassie asked sceptically. 'So, what, you slept with her, left as usual, and now you're, what? Missing her?' She shook her head. 'You're such an idiot.'

'Thanks for the pep talk.' His little sister always did know how to kick a guy when he was down. At least, that was what her first husband had said. Her second hadn't commented on it so far. Dylan liked him a lot more than the first.

'Seriously, Dyl, when are you going to stop running before you even have a chance to see if there could be something there?' Cassie waved her bottle at him accusingly. 'You're always the same. You find someone you like, indulge in a fling or whatever, then walk away before it can go anywhere. And this time it really looks like it could have! I haven't seen you this bummed since that deal in London went wrong.'

'What's the point in staying?' Dylan asked. 'I mean, we all know that I'll be leaving eventually, right? When the next big opportunity comes up, I'll be on my way. Why make that harder than it has to be?' He couldn't even deny the accusations Sadie had thrown at him. He didn't stay—and she wouldn't go. Permanent mismatch.

'That's just horse droppings!'

'You've been watching your language around kids too long.'

'I'd use stronger if I thought it would make you listen!' Cassie sighed, and settled onto the edge of her chair, staring earnestly up at him. 'Did you even think about staying and fighting for her? That's what you do, you know, when you love someone. You stay and figure things out. Every morning you wake up and decide to try harder. That's all there is to it.'

'She told me to leave. She has a son…commitments. There was no place for me there.' Even if it had felt, just for a moment, like he could have fitted into their lives perfectly.

'Honestly, Dyl, if you believe that you're stupider than even I ever thought. Just because Dad left doesn't mean you will. Of course you can settle down, *of course* you can commit, when you find the right thing.'

'And how, exactly, do you know that?' Because he sure didn't.

'Because you've already done it once.' Cassie sat back in her chair, a smug look on her face.

Dylan blinked. 'How do you mean?'

'You did it for me and Mum. You spent years taking care of us, committed to making sure we were okay even when we went out of our way to mess that up.' She smiled gently at him, and Dylan felt some of the truth of her words sink into his bones. 'You never thought about walking away, did you?'

'No. I suppose I didn't.'

'And you've never stopped either. You still check up on us both. You're always there for my boys—and I know you always will be. That's why I named you their guardian in my will.'

'You did?' Why hadn't he known that? Unless Cassie

had thought the idea of it would have freaked him out. Which, before this week, it probably would have.

Cassie nodded. 'Too right. I wouldn't trust anyone else with them.'

'Thanks. I think.'

'And I bet we're not the only ones,' Cassie went on. 'What about your friends? I mean, you said you went out there to help this old friend out. You've always done that, too. Whatever your friends needed, you were there. That's commitment too, you know.'

'I never thought of it that way,' Dylan admitted. All those years, he'd committed to the people who mattered to him—his friends and family.

The truth struck him hard in the chest. Friends and family? Sadie was already both, in his heart.

He was already committed, and he hadn't even noticed.

Now he just needed to convince her of that.

Maybe he wasn't Adem. But maybe he could be what she needed now instead.

And maybe, just maybe, he could be what Finn needed too. After all, he knew better than anyone how fundamental having a father figure in a boy's life could be. Maybe he could even give Finn what he and Cassie had lost when he had been ten.

Cassie took another swig of her beer. 'Little sisters are always right, you know. So, need me to book you a ticket to Turkey?'

But Dylan was already on the phone to the airline.

Sadie hung back from the gravestone, flowers held awkwardly in her hands. Her dad was waiting in the car with Finn, ready to take them back to the airport, so she didn't have long. But coming to the churchyard had seemed like the right thing to do before she left.

But now she was here, staring at a stone that spoke about a beloved father, son, husband and friend, she didn't know what to do next.

Adem wasn't here, not for her. She knew his parents felt better having him close, but for her no motionless, cold stone could ever represent her warm, loving, enthusiastic husband. She felt his presence far more in the heat of a Turkish summer or in the halls and rooms of the Azure.

And maybe that was why she needed to be here. To ask for his blessing, or advice, or something. To tell him that she needed to move on at last.

'I'll always love you,' she said, placing the flowers carefully by the stone. 'But I think you know that anyway.' She'd told him often enough in life.

Sighing, she crouched down in front of the flowers. 'We had a wonderful life together, didn't we? And we made the most precious little boy. But…I don't think you'd want me to stay in this limbo. And I'm starting to think I can't.'

She swallowed, fighting back the tears that pooled in the corners of her eyes. 'I need to move on. I'm not quite sure what to yet, but I don't think that matters as much as being ready to take the chances as they come.'

Just because Dylan wasn't an opportunity it didn't mean there wouldn't be others. In work, as well as in love.

'You always said that your instincts were the most important compass you had,' she went on. 'That if you trusted your instincts nothing much could go wrong. You said…' A choked sob escaped her throat. 'You said that asking me to marry you when we were so young, with no prospects, was the biggest ever test of that. And me saying yes…that was the last time I truly trusted my own instincts instead of yours.

'Well, that changes now. I don't know what's going

to happen next but… Dylan's assistant called. We have the investment we need to save the Azure. So I'm going to make that happen and then I'm going to find someone I trust to manage the place when I'm away. I'll take Finn back often, I promise, and it will be there for him when he's old enough. But in the meantime my instincts tell me we should be here, in England, with our families. And then…well, I guess we'll see. I have faith that the right thing will come along at the right time.' She managed a lopsided smile. 'It always did for you after all. Until the last.'

Adem's life had been too short and their happiness cut off before its time. But the happiness they'd had together would be hers to treasure for always. And she would.

Kissing her fingers, she pressed them against the stone. 'Love you,' she whispered.

Then, wiping her eyes, she turned and headed back towards the car, and her future.

CHAPTER SIXTEEN

SADIE SIGHED WITH relief as the car from the airport turned up the road that led to the Azure Hotel.

'Nearly there,' she told Finn, who snuggled down further on his booster seat, arms wrapped around his favourite teddy. 'Nearly home.'

Home for now, anyway.

The flight had been long and tedious, with a change in Istanbul that had dragged on as they'd waited for a delayed plane. Finn had been brilliant, really, but the journey had been trying for *her,* let alone a four-year-old. Still, with the help of plenty of snacks, a new toy or two saved for the occasion, and a well-timed nap on the last leg, they'd made it.

If nothing else, all the time in transit had given her time to think—to start to form plans, ideas that she hoped would come together as the weeks went on.

She was returning to Turkey prepared for her fresh start, ready to jump at the right opportunities as they presented themselves.

Of course, some sign as to what the right opportunities were would be appreciated, but Sadie figured that was part of trusting her instincts—figuring that out for herself.

'We're here,' she whispered to Finn as the car drew to

a halt. He blinked at her a couple of times then opened his eyes wider.

'The Azure?'

'That's right. You ready to get back to your room and your things? I know Esma's been missing you.'

Sadie opened the door and let him hop out onto the pavement, following as the driver retrieved their bags.

'Thanks,' she said, stopping for a moment to look up at her hotel. *Her* hotel. She liked the sound of that.

The familiar Azure sign shone above the glass doors and she smiled at it as she lowered her gaze…and felt her heart stop.

As Esma rushed out and tried to whisk Finn away, chattering loudly about milkshakes and special sweet bread in the kitchens, Sadie stared at the man standing under the Azure sign.

Dylan Jacobs.

Well, she'd asked for a sign.

'What are you doing here?' She stepped closer, leaving her bags on the pavement as the car pulled away.

'Mum?' Finn asked, looking between her and Dylan. Esma shot Sadie an apologetic look. 'Who's this?'

Dylan crouched down beside Finn and the smile on his face was a new one to Sadie. Friendly, warm and with no edge, no demands. No business.

'You probably don't remember me, but I was one of your dad's best friends.'

'You knew my dad?' Finn's face scrunched up, just a little. 'If you were friends with Dad and Uncle Neal, are you Dylan?'

Dylan held out his hand. 'Dylan Jacobs. At your service.'

Finn shook his hand solemnly, his fingers tiny around Dylan's bigger ones, and Sadie felt her heart contract at the sight. 'Uncle Neal tells me stories about you and Dad sometimes. How come you never come and see us, like he does?'

'I've been…' Dylan trailed off before he could finish the sentence, but Sadie was pretty sure the missing words were 'too busy with work'. Wasn't that always the case? But then he started again.

'I'm sorry, Finn. I should have done. I should have visited more. And I'd like to start now, if that's okay with you.'

'I guess so.' Finn tilted his head to the side. 'Do you like milkshakes?'

'Love them.' Dylan grinned. 'Maybe we can grab one together later? After I speak to your mum?'

Finn nodded. 'Okay.' Esma took his arm again and this time he didn't object as she led him off to the kitchens. Sadie sighed with relief—until she realised that left her alone with Dylan.

Just what she was trying to avoid. 'There's really no need for you to be here,' she said. 'I told your assistant I'd get the forms to him by—'

Dylan shook his head to stop her, standing up from his crouch. 'I'm not here in a professional capacity.'

How she'd missed that voice. Warm and smooth and caressing—even when he was chatting with Finn or when they were talking business. Just seeing him again made her want to reach out and grab him, to hold on and never let him go.

This was why she'd needed not to see him again. When she was near him it was impossible to deny that she'd fallen ridiculously in love with him.

'Then why are you here?' she managed to ask through her muddled thoughts.

Dylan stepped closer, taking a breath so deep she saw his chest move under his shirt. 'I'm here to commit.'

'To what?' Sadie asked, blinking. Because he couldn't possibly mean what she thought he did. Could he?

'To whatever you need to be happy,' Dylan replied. 'If that's me thousands of miles away, then I'll commit to that. If it's still the Azure, I'll work like the devil to make that happen with you. If it's England with Finn, I can make that work too. All I want is a chance. A chance to prove that I can be part of your plan, of your future.'

'That's it?' Was this really the same man who had walked out on her in such a fury?

'That's it,' Dylan confirmed. 'I know I'm not Adem, and I never will be. But I can be more than you think of me. All I want is a chance to be with you, however you need me. To be there for you and Finn. And I know that can't happen all of a sudden—he needs to get used to me, we need to figure out things between us... So, a new proposal, okay? No jumping in feet first, just a slow, measured plan you can back out of any time you want. The sort of plan you like, I promise.'

The ultimate commitment-phobe was offering to commit. The man who *always* leapt at the next big thing was promising to stick to just one plan. Her plan.

Hope blossomed deep in Sadie's chest, like the cherry tree in her parents' back garden in England, flowering with hope and possibility in the spring.

But... She shook her head. 'I'm sorry, Dylan. That won't work for me.'

That was it. With just those few words she'd dashed any hope Dylan had ever had of committing again, he was sure. The heaviness in his chest sank lower and lower until...

He blinked. Was she smiling?

Sadie stepped closer and he let just a little chink of hope back in.

'This time…' she said, reaching up to place her hand against his cheek. 'This time I'm trusting my instincts. I'm taking all the opportunities I can to be truly happy again. And I think I know what that means, at last.'

'You do?' Then he wished to God she'd tell him because he had no idea what was going on.

Sadie nodded. 'I want Finn to have the Azure when he's older, but I don't want to run it myself. Once we've got things set up here and on the road to recovery, I'm hoping you'll help me find a manager we can trust so that Finn and I can move back to England.'

'Of course. Does that mean you've reconsidered my job offer?' Was this business? Or pleasure? Her closeness suggested the latter, but her words didn't. And he'd already been caught out by that before.

'I've reconsidered a lot of things,' she admitted. 'I want to run my own spas, I know that. And if we can work together on that…well, that would be great.'

'That all sounds good,' Dylan said cautiously.

'But that's not all,' Sadie went on. 'I'm afraid I'm greedy. I want more than just my family near, my son happy and a dream business. I want you, too.'

His heart stopped, just for a moment. 'I thought you said—'

'I said that slow and measured wasn't going to work for me any more,' Sadie corrected him. 'I know we can't rush too much officially because of Finn—I need to be sure that he's ready for there to be someone else in my life, and that he's happy for it to be you. So, officially, fine, we go with your plan.'

'But unofficially?' He didn't care. He'd say yes to anything right now if it meant being part of her life. Hers and Finn's.

'Life's too short, I've seen that first hand. You have to take your chances for happiness when they come. So just between you and me… I hope you were serious about wanting to commit…'

'I was,' Dylan assured her.

'Good. Because…' She took a deep breath. 'Dylan Jacobs, will you marry me?'

Pure joy spread through his body at her words. This was one opportunity he had no intention of missing.

Reaching into his pocket, he pulled out the ring box he'd acquired in Sydney and flipped it open between them. 'Great minds?' he said, as Sadie laughed.

'I should have known the slow-and-steady thing was a bluff.' She took the ring from the box and stared at the diamond, mesmerised. 'You never did anything that way in your life.'

'Oh, I don't know,' Dylan said, as he slid the ring onto her finger. 'It took me thirteen years to find the right woman to commit to.'

'But now you're sure?' Sadie asked.

'I'm beyond certain,' Dylan promised, leaning in to kiss all her doubts away. 'You're my next, last and only big thing. Your love is the only thing that matters to me. You, Finn and I are going to be the happiest little family ever, I'm committed to that. And I plan to spend the rest of my life proving it to you.'

Sadie smiled, and kissed him back.

And in that moment Dylan knew, bone deep, that proposing to Sadie was worth more than the chance at any million-dollar business deal, and that marrying her would give him more opportunities for happiness than one man could ever use in a lifetime.

EPILOGUE

CHERRY BLOSSOMS BLEW across the garden from the tree at the far end, and Sadie watched, smiling, as Finn tried to catch them, Dylan swinging him up in his arms to reach higher.

In the kitchen behind her, her parents were putting the finishing touches to a Sunday roast—and didn't need any help at all, thank you. Ordered to relax, Sadie had retired to the garden to enjoy the spring sunshine and just be with her family. At any minute her sister would arrive with her brood, and they'd all be together.

In the six months since Dylan had first arrived at the Azure, life had changed beyond recognition—and into something Sadie had never even hoped for. It hadn't all been easy, and business had intruded more than she'd have liked. But Finn had taken to Dylan instantly—and his awed admiration seemed to be reciprocated. Some nights, when Dylan was staying with them—always in the spare room, as far as Finn was concerned—she'd catch Dylan sneaking into Finn's room just to watch him sleeping. The amazed love in his eyes always made her want to kiss him harder.

They'd finally broached the topic of becoming a real family with Finn the weekend before, despite Sadie's anxieties. His little five-year-old nose had scrunched up at the idea.

'So, Dylan would live with us?' he'd asked.

'When he didn't have to travel for work, yes,' Sadie had answered nervously.

'Good. I like our house. I can walk to Grandma and Granddad's from here, and to school, and Phoebe and CJ can visit me lots.' Dylan had shared a small smile with her at that. When she'd tried to insist on finding a place to rent on her own, maybe in Oxford, he'd pointed out that she'd only have to move again in a few months when they finally let everyone else in on their engagement. The whole point was to be near her family—so together they'd found the perfect house just across the village from her parents'.

It already felt like home should.

'So, you wouldn't mind me marrying your mum?' Dylan had asked, and Sadie had heard the nerves in his voice even if Finn hadn't. He'd come such a long way from the man she remembered as Adem's friend. And he was so much more now, to her and to Finn.

'Will I have to wear a stupid suit?' Finn had asked. 'My friend Riley did when his mum got married.'

'You can wear whatever you like,' Dylan had promised, his relief obvious.

Finn had tipped his head to the side, studied Dylan for a moment, then clambered up into his lap for a hug. 'Then I think it would be pretty great.'

As far as Sadie was concerned, it already was.

A commotion came from behind her and Sadie knew that Rachel had arrived with the kids. Finn came running towards her, cherry blossoms forgotten, Dylan following. As he passed, Sadie grabbed Finn around his waist and pulled him up into her lap.

'Mum!' He wiggled, trying to escape. 'CJ and Phoebe are here!'

'I know,' Sadie said. 'So, how would you like to be the one to tell everyone the big news?'

'The wedding news?' Finn whispered conspiratorially.

Sadie nodded, smiling at Dylan over Finn's head.

'Okay!' He jumped down and ran into the house. 'Guess what, everybody! Mum and Dylan are getting married!'

Dylan held out a hand to pull her to her feet. 'Better put this on, then.' He fished in his pocket for a familiar-looking ring box and handed it to her. 'It'll be good to see it on your hand permanently at last.'

'It'll be good to wear it.' She let him slide the ring into place then reached up to kiss him as her mum's squeals of joy rang out from inside.

'When do you propose to tell them our other news?' Dylan murmured against her mouth, his hand brushing across her middle.

'We've got a few weeks yet,' Sadie whispered back. 'Let's let this one sink in first.' In truth, she was enjoying the secret. 'Besides, I want Finn to know before anyone else. Being a big brother is a big job.'

'That it is.' He kissed her again, and Sadie felt a warmth flow through her that had more to do with love than spring sunshine and cherry blossom.

She was home at last, exactly where she was meant to be, and all her plans for the future looked golden.

* * * * *

MILLS & BOON®
Hardback – October 2015

ROMANCE

Claimed for Makarov's Baby	Sharon Kendrick
An Heir Fit for a King	Abby Green
The Wedding Night Debt	Cathy Williams
Seducing His Enemy's Daughter	Annie West
Reunited for the Billionaire's Legacy	Jennifer Hayward
Hidden in the Sheikh's Harem	Michelle Conder
Resisting the Sicilian Playboy	Amanda Cinelli
The Return of Antonides	Anne McAllister
Soldier, Hero...Husband?	Cara Colter
Falling for Mr December	Kate Hardy
The Baby Who Saved Christmas	Alison Roberts
A Proposal Worth Millions	Sophie Pembroke
The Baby of Their Dreams	Carol Marinelli
Falling for Her Reluctant Sheikh	Amalie Berlin
Hot-Shot Doc, Secret Dad	Lynne Marshall
Father for Her Newborn Baby	Lynne Marshall
His Little Christmas Miracle	Emily Forbes
Safe in the Surgeon's Arms	Molly Evans
Pursued	Tracy Wolff
A Royal Temptation	Charlene Sands

MILLS & BOON®
Large Print – October 2015

ROMANCE

The Bride Fonseca Needs	Abby Green
Sheikh's Forbidden Conquest	Chantelle Shaw
Protecting the Desert Heir	Caitlin Crews
Seduced into the Greek's World	Dani Collins
Tempted by Her Billionaire Boss	Jennifer Hayward
Married for the Prince's Convenience	Maya Blake
The Sicilian's Surprise Wife	Tara Pammi
His Unexpected Baby Bombshell	Soraya Lane
Falling for the Bridesmaid	Sophie Pembroke
A Millionaire for Cinderella	Barbara Wallace
From Paradise...to Pregnant!	Kandy Shepherd

HISTORICAL

A Mistress for Major Bartlett	Annie Burrows
The Chaperon's Seduction	Sarah Mallory
Rake Most Likely to Rebel	Bronwyn Scott
Whispers at Court	Blythe Gifford
Summer of the Viking	Michelle Styles

MEDICAL

Just One Night?	Carol Marinelli
Meant-To-Be Family	Marion Lennox
The Soldier She Could Never Forget	Tina Beckett
The Doctor's Redemption	Susan Carlisle
Wanted: Parents for a Baby!	Laura Iding
His Perfect Bride?	Louisa Heaton

MILLS & BOON®
Hardback – November 2015

ROMANCE

A Christmas Vow of Seduction	Maisey Yates
Brazilian's Nine Months' Notice	Susan Stephens
The Sheikh's Christmas Conquest	Sharon Kendrick
Shackled to the Sheikh	Trish Morey
Unwrapping the Castelli Secret	Caitlin Crews
A Marriage Fit for a Sinner	Maya Blake
Larenzo's Christmas Baby	Kate Hewitt
Bought for Her Innocence	Tara Pammi
His Lost-and-Found Bride	Scarlet Wilson
Housekeeper Under the Mistletoe	Cara Colter
Gift-Wrapped in Her Wedding Dress	Kandy Shepherd
The Prince's Christmas Vow	Jennifer Faye
A Touch of Christmas Magic	Scarlet Wilson
Her Christmas Baby Bump	Robin Gianna
Winter Wedding in Vegas	Janice Lynn
One Night Before Christmas	Susan Carlisle
A December to Remember	Sue MacKay
A Father This Christmas?	Louisa Heaton
A Christmas Baby Surprise	Catherine Mann
Courting the Cowboy Boss	Janice Maynard

MILLS & BOON

Large Print – November 2015

ROMANCE

The Ruthless Greek's Return	Sharon Kendrick
Bound by the Billionaire's Baby	Cathy Williams
Married for Amari's Heir	Maisey Yates
A Taste of Sin	Maggie Cox
Sicilian's Shock Proposal	Carol Marinelli
Vows Made in Secret	Louise Fuller
The Sheikh's Wedding Contract	Andie Brock
A Bride for the Italian Boss	Susan Meier
The Millionaire's True Worth	Rebecca Winters
The Earl's Convenient Wife	Marion Lennox
Vettori's Damsel in Distress	Liz Fielding

HISTORICAL

A Rose for Major Flint	Louise Allen
The Duke's Daring Debutante	Ann Lethbridge
Lord Laughraine's Summer Promise	Elizabeth Beacon
Warrior of Ice	Michelle Willingham
A Wager for the Widow	Elisabeth Hobbes

MEDICAL

Always the Midwife	Alison Roberts
Midwife's Baby Bump	Susanne Hampton
A Kiss to Melt Her Heart	Emily Forbes
Tempted by Her Italian Surgeon	Louisa George
Daring to Date Her Ex	Annie Claydon
The One Man to Heal Her	Meredith Webber

MILLS & BOON®

Why shop at millsandboon.co.uk?

Each year, thousands of romance readers find their perfect read at millsandboon.co.uk. That's because we're passionate about bringing you the very best romantic fiction. Here are some of the advantages of shopping at www.millsandboon.co.uk:

* **Get new books first**—you'll be able to buy your favourite books one month before they hit the shops

* **Get exclusive discounts**—you'll also be able to buy our specially created monthly collections, with up to 50% off the RRP

* **Find your favourite authors**—latest news, interviews and new releases for all your favourite authors and series on our website, plus ideas for what to try next

* **Join in**—once you've bought your favourite books, don't forget to register with us to rate, review and join in the discussions

Visit **www.millsandboon.co.uk**
for all this and more today!